MASTER BY FATE

MA INNES

1

COOPER

"DATE. DATE. DATE. PANCAKES. DATE. SEX." Bouncing around the kitchen, I tried to remember everything I was supposed to do. It was my turn to clean the kitchen, and I wanted to get it all done before I went to work.

But I knew I'd forgotten something.

"Cooper!" Sawyer's frustration made me smile, and I looked over toward the fridge where he was standing, trying to dig his lunch out of the back of it. That was what I was supposed to have been doing...clearing out the old stuff.

Giving him a sweet smile, I cocked my head innocently. "Yes?"

He snorted and crouched to grab the plastic container of leftovers. "You're making me crazy."

"Because you want pancakes too?" It was date night with Jackson, and I couldn't wait.

"No, because you've been talking to yourself all morning about the date." He rolled his eyes as he stood.

He was no fun today.

"I'm excited."

"No, you were excited when you were just talking about

your date…but singing about it crosses the line." Sawyer closed the refrigerator and started checking to make sure he'd remembered everything.

"I wasn't singing." I'd just been cheerful.

He was grumpy because he didn't want to go to the dinner meeting. Trying to look calmer so I didn't push him any closer to the edge, I walked over to Sawyer and threw my arms around him. "It's going to be fine. They wouldn't have invited you along if they didn't think you'd do a good job."

In the past, Sawyer hadn't gotten involved in the new projects until the contracts had been signed and all the details laid out. He wasn't sure if it was because his boss's daughter was working with Jackson or because he'd been doing a good job, but they'd been giving him more responsibilities lately, and it made him uncomfortable.

It was probably just his worries about work and the stress of moving in with Jackson, but lately Sawyer looked like he needed a vacation. It wasn't that living with Jackson was difficult. Really, it'd been an easier transition than when Sawyer and I had moved into our first apartment, but I knew the change and the constant what-ifs running through his head had his tension running high.

Sawyer smiled when I grinned and waggled my eyebrows. "I'm sure Master and I can think up some interesting ways to help you relax this weekend."

What he didn't know was that we'd already had it planned out. Sawyer was going to have a perfect weekend. He leaned in and gave me a kiss. "I'm sure you can, Coop. Okay, I have to go, but I'll try to text you at least before your shift. Have fun on your date if I don't get to talk to you later."

"Love you, and of course I'll have fun. It's sex and pancakes. It's going to be fabulous." That should have gone without saying. "You stop worrying. It's dinner with dull people who are going to talk about plants and numbers. You'll probably die of boredom before you even have to order. Oh wait, you like math and plants....You'll have fun then. Not as much fun as sex and pancakes, but then, that's hard to beat."

Sawyer laughed and gave me a tender kiss. "You're right. That's difficult to top."

Grinning, I nodded excitedly. "I told you so."

My date was going to be great. Jackson had even said he had a surprise for me. I was hoping it was a naughty one. Jackson gave the best naughty surprises. Still smiling, Sawyer stepped away after giving me a quick peck. "Okay, I have to go, but behave for your date, and I'll see you tonight."

"Let us know if you're going to be late." Jackson's voice came from the kitchen doorway, making us both jump. He laughed and shook his head. "You both look very guilty."

I widened my eyes and shook my head. "Sawyer did it."

Jackson laughed. "Of course he did, pup. What did he do?"

I whispered like it was absolutely scandalous and leaned in close. "He worried and didn't tell you."

Jackson nodded, clearly understanding the gravity of the situation. Sawyer watched us both and shook his head like we were nuts. "Oh, you're right. He was naughty. I think we're going to have to figure out a punishment for him later."

"I agree." I shrugged and gave Sawyer a pitiful look. "Master will make sure you learn your lesson."

Oh, yes...Master was going to make sure Sawyer had fun and let go of his worries for the weekend.

Sawyer tried to look innocent, but it wasn't good enough. The laughter in his eyes was poking through. "I'm not the one who hasn't finished their portion of the chores. He's been in here all morning, and it's only half-done."

Okay, in my defense, this kitchen was bigger than the old apartment's and we actually used it. That made *everything* take longer.

And then there was my date tonight.

And the fact that cleaning the kitchen was *so* boring.

Jackson chuckled and glanced around the kitchen but didn't say anything about the half-cleaned room. It wasn't *that* bad. Focusing his attention back on Sawyer, he shook his head dramatically. "I think that's tattling. Cooper's right. We have to help you remember how to be good."

Ha!

Stepping back from Sawyer, I grinned and glanced at the clock on the stove. "He's also going to be late if he doesn't get going. So naughty today."

Sawyer rolled his eyes and tried to seem calm, but I could see his excitement building. The way he shifted his weight from one foot to the other looked like he was trying to discreetly adjust his cock. Someone was anticipating being punished.

"Come on. I'll walk you out to the car." Jackson smiled and moved toward Sawyer, wrapping one arm around his waist as they headed to the back door.

They were so cute together.

Sawyer leaned into his touch, and the rest of the stress he'd been holding seemed to melt away. We were the perfect pair for Sawyer. I could tease him and distract him with fabulous things. Then Jackson could push the rest of it away with that calming touch that made us both want to curl into him and let the rest of the world fade into nothingness.

As they headed out the back door, I gave up pretending to clean the kitchen and went over to peek out the window. They were even cuter. Jackson was leaning back against the car with Sawyer wrapped in his arms. Sawyer was holding his lunch and his bag but curled into Jackson like it was the safest place in the world.

My men were so perfect together.

Jackson was running his hand over Sawyer's back, and though I couldn't hear it, I knew he was talking low and tender. It was exactly what Sawyer needed to get back into the right headspace for work. After a few minutes, maybe not even that long, Sawyer straightened and nodded at whatever Jackson had said. Leaning in, he gave Jackson a quick kiss and then pointed toward the house, smiling.

Oops.

Heading back to the fridge, I started cleaning out the weird stuff that had accumulated over the past couple of days. We did a lot of the cleaning after dinner, so technically this wasn't supposed to be that hard of a job, but it was just terrible. Throwing away leftovers and working through the rest of the list was boring.

But with three people living together, even I had to admit hiring someone wasn't practical. Not that I hadn't tried to bribe Jackson and Sawyer into at least considering the idea. The closest I'd gotten was that if we won the lottery, we could hire someone to help out around the place.

They were going to regret that when I actually won, because I was going to hold 'em to it.

Jackson came back in, chuckling. "Peeping Tom."

"It doesn't count when it's you guys. You both like to be watched." I shrugged and looked over my shoulder to give him a grin. "And I was very subtle, so you had alone time."

Jackson walked over and pulled me away from the fridge and into his arms. "Yes, you were."

Giving me a quick kiss, he smiled. "Are you excited about tonight?"

"Yes. Pancakes and sex!" It was going to be the best date night ever.

Making sure we got time as couples and not just with all three of us together was important to Jackson. He'd even sent Sawyer and me to the movies the other night, so we could have a date while he stayed home to do some paperwork. I understood why it was important to him, and I appreciated how thoughtful he was, but I liked having him there with us.

Having him around felt right—probably because we'd been waiting so long to find the perfect person who would understand us. Eventually, I'd appreciate his insistence, but I was still at the point where I wanted to tie myself to him and make sure he couldn't escape.

"Yes, pancakes and then we can play. Do you know what you want to do?" Jackson had said we could do whatever I picked for our date and for our time together, but there were too many fabulous options to choose.

"No…" Then a thought occurred to me. I pressed myself tighter against him and looked at him innocently. "But I'm sure you can show me all kinds of interesting things. I've been very sheltered, Sir."

Jackson's smile turned heated, but there was also laughter in his eyes that made me want to say more outrageous things just to make him laugh out loud. "I know it's going to be your first date, my boy, but I'll take care of you."

Yes!

"Thank you, Sir. I want to be a good boy for you, so you'll be excited to see me again. I don't want this to be our only date." Oh no, I wanted lots of sexy, fun role-play time with him in the future.

We hadn't gotten to play much with sexy fantasies, but even the little bit we'd done had been enough to make Jackson more turned on than ever. I was going to be his sexy boy out for the first time with a man…and eventually, beg him to take me.

He'd love it.

Hell, we'd both love it.

I was going to have so many fabulous things to tell Sawyer when he got home.

Desire radiated from Jackson, and all I wanted to do was press myself against him harder and rub my cock along his. When he spoke, I could almost hear the naughty fantasies running through his head. "I know you're going to be a good boy for me. As long as you're very obedient, we'll have lots of dates."

Jackson's hands moved down my back to cup my ass. "I have lots of new things to show you."

"But what happens if I'm naughty? I don't want you to be mad." Sweet or naughty...it was such a hard decision.

"If you don't want me to be mad, and you don't want our dates to end, then I would have to punish you to make sure you remember how to be good the next time." His fingers kneaded and pulled my cheeks apart just enough for me to imagine him filling my ass with his dick. It was maddening. "Don't you want there to be a next time...even if you're a naughty boy?"

My hips thrust forward, grinding my cock against his.

Bad cock.

"Yes, please." I licked my lips and looked up at him, not trying to deny how much I wanted him but cloaking it all in a layer of sexy innocence. "I want to make you happy, Sir, and if that means punishing me when I'm bad, then I want you to do that."

Jackson finally broke.

His hands rocked my hips to rub my dick against his, and his mouth came down to take mine. He poured every bit of need and love into me as he took my mouth. When he finally pulled away, he smiled down at me. "You are pure temptation."

I wiggled against him. "I'm not just tempting you....I'm actually going to give it to you...or let you take it, if that would be more fun."

Jackson laughed and gave me a peck on the lips. "You have work in a little while." Then he glanced around the kitchen, grinning. "And the rest of the cleaning to finish. I, on the other hand, have to fold the laundry before I start on updating the website."

Sighing, I looked around the kitchen. I'd rather be folding

laundry, even if that included remaking the bed and cleaning the sheets. "That's not as much fun as my idea."

Jackson's smile turned loving and playful. "You always have much better ideas. But we agreed to do the chores, and I have a feeling that Sawyer will be frustrated with us both if I let you distract me every time we're supposed to clean."

"It was just once." Distract someone with a blowjob one time when you were supposed to be vacuuming, and no one ever let you forget it.

Jackson shook his head trying not to laugh. "Three times, Cooper."

"It couldn't have been." Could it?

Jackson pulled away enough that we were no longer pressed together and started counting on one hand. "The blowjob in the living room...the shower sex...the kitchen table."

Okay, Sawyer might kill me then. "I'm buying a lottery ticket on the way to work."

Laughing, Jackson gave my ass a pat and stepped away completely. "I had a feeling you'd say that."

Sighing dramatically as Jackson walked out of the kitchen, I tried to remember what I'd been doing before he'd interrupted me. The dishwasher? The stove?

"There have to be ways of making this more fun." There just had to. "The fridge!"

Because, *duh*, I was standing next to it. If anyone needed to get in trouble for me not finishing, it was Jackson. Opening the fridge, I bent over and started digging through the shelves, trying to decide what to throw out. Then it hit me. "Oh...that's going to be perfect."

I could make *anything* fun and fabulous.

2

SAWYER

COOPER CLEANED the kitchen like an ADHD squirrel.

It was almost frightening. He bounced from one side of the room to the other, never quite finishing a project before he bounced on to something else and then back to the last project. It was one of the reasons we'd done a lot of the chores together before; sometimes he just needed someone to keep him on track.

But Jackson had been right. With a bigger house and three people who all worked different shifts, it would be almost impossible for us to do everything together. But I thought we were going to have to work out a different system for the chores. There were other things Cooper liked doing better, ones that held his attention.

Next time we all sat down to figure out our schedules and the things that were coming up, I'd talk about it with Jackson. The meetings were actually a good idea, but I still thought the whole thing was humorous. Everyone wanted to make the new living arrangements work, but sometimes it felt like we were trying too hard.

As I pulled away from the house, I glanced at the rear-view mirror. Seeing it get smaller made my heart clench. Everything had happened so quickly, but it had easily become our home. It wasn't because it was bigger or nicer. No, it wasn't something as tangible as that. Part of it was because it was where Jackson was. Cooper wasn't the only one who liked being close to Master. It was more than that, though. Something about the space felt like we'd finally found where we belonged.

That hadn't meant all the changes had been easy. Looking back, I could see Cooper's and Jackson's hands in working out some of the details like who would get the cars when, before we'd even started talking about moving in together.

I knew we needed some time to let things smooth out. It was nice not to have the fear and panic pressing down on us like it had been when Cooper and I had become a family. In those days, there had been more panic than joy. But with Jackson, I'd been able to just enjoy having everyone together. Waking and knowing that both of my men were beside me was wonderful.

There were so many changes at once.

Everything would've been easier if at least one part of my life had stayed consistent. Work had never been monotonous, but even when the projects changed it had a familiar feel to it. Lately, though, it had lost that familiarity.

More responsibilities and input weren't necessarily a bad thing. I just wished it had happened later down the road. Maybe then I would've believed I'd earned it. But with everything happening so close together, I wasn't sure why my boss had started treating me differently.

Not that I would complain about finally being listened to. Or maybe I *was* complaining.

Either way, I loved that I was being given the chance to voice my opinions. In the past, we'd done projects that had been good, but there'd been parts of them I would've changed. When I first started working for the company, I'd been grateful for the opportunity to take my career in a different direction. Providing for Cooper had been my only goal. But as time had gone on, there had been a part of me that had wanted to be seen as a success.

I just hadn't expected it would take introducing my boss to my two boyfriends to get noticed.

Cooper thought it was because I started opening up at the company, and that had shown I was taking my job more seriously. Jackson said a lot of companies liked to see their workers settled down and happy before they got promoted, because they had a better chance of keeping employees longer that way. I thought it had something to do with the boss's daughter working for Jackson, but I couldn't be sure.

Aside from the fact that I actually thought I deserved the promotion. When I considered it objectively, I felt some of it had to do with my boss's gratitude for his daughter's happiness. Having someone that accepted her and understood her had made a world of difference. At least from the things her father had mentioned.

I tried to stay out of it. She was starting to feel like a friend of mine and I didn't want to come between them, but her dad didn't seem to understand. Jackson said it was probably a relief for him that he had someone to talk about it with. I just saw it as too much information-sharing in the workplace and that we needed to focus on our actual jobs.

And maybe that was what else had gotten me more responsibility?

I wished I understood where the changes at work would take me. The company was small, and turnover was low enough that very few people in the office ever left. Accounts were traded occasionally between managers, but that was about it.

None of the other assistants had ever been invited to dinner before—and certainly never before the details had been worked out and the contract signed. Normally, I wouldn't have been given any information until the basic requirements of the client had been laid out. I liked the idea of coming in early, so I could really understand what the clients needed, but it was concerning.

I wasn't sure if I would fit in. I was probably ten years younger than any of the managers, and realistically, I could have been my boss's kid. I didn't want to look like the baby at the table who was too stupid to know how to speak and what manners to use. I'd basically grown up with white trash parents, and my elementary school teachers had been the first people I could remember who'd ever pointed out manners.

I kept telling myself that someone would have said something if what I'd been doing had been embarrassing or offensive in the past, but I wasn't sure. Jackson had never said I'd embarrassed him in public or that I'd needed to fix something before he could introduce me to his family. So I hoped that meant I wouldn't embarrass myself at dinner. I just wasn't confident enough to believe it yet.

As I headed toward the interstate to go downtown, I tried to take a few deep breaths. When that didn't work, I started fiddling with the radio buttons. Cooper had done his best to ease my stress, and so had Jackson; I wished I could have carried their confidence around with me in my pocket.

I WAS THE FUCKIN' TOKEN GAY GUY — AT LEAST, THAT WAS how it was starting to look.

I hadn't been able to get any specific information on why I'd been included, but as introductions started being made, it became clearer. Several managers from our company, as well as the owner, attended the dinner to meet the prospective client. Greg Sanders was probably in his late forties with a strong presence and a *husband*.

My boss was inept enough at dealing with his daughter that I understood why he might have wanted someone else with him at the dinner. It wouldn't have been a good idea to have him in charge of the conversation. On some level, I was glad he understood that, because it meant he was making progress with her. But surely, one of the other managers could make a good impression.

It was evidently a big enough project that no one wanted to risk it, however. As we sat down around the long table, the conversation was stilted. My introduction had been slightly vague. After giving my name, they'd mentioned that if everything worked out, I would be involved in their project.

They'd just left out the part about me being an assistant.

Gregory Spencer and his husband Chris were polite but clearly unimpressed with the awkwardness. Looking at it from their angle, they probably saw us as a group of homophobic assholes, but there was no good way to point out that I was surrounded by morons.

It was also no accident that I'd been seated across from the couple, so I decided to make the best of it. There was no reason to make the men uncomfortable, although my boss would get an earful when I got him alone. Smiling at Chris, I tried to think of something to say. If I'd been given a little bit of notice, I might have at least been able to figure out what he did for a living. "So are you involved in the development?"

Chris looked slightly relieved but shook his head. "No, thank goodness." Then he glanced over at Gregory and gave him a smile. "We wouldn't have lasted six months working together."

Chuckling, I nodded. "I can understand that. My partner owns his own business and we live onsite. So there's never any separation of work and home life."

They both relaxed more in their seats and gave me more attention. It was Chris's turn to chuckle. "He must be more laid-back than this one. We've had to make strict rules about how much work can come home."

I smiled. "I wouldn't exactly describe Jackson as laid-back, but it takes a lot to get him worked up, and he's very focused on being present when he's at home. Unless he has to catch up on bills—then we avoid him like the plague."

They both laughed, nodding. Gregory glanced at Chris, looking slightly guilty. "Oh, I remember the days of having to do all the accounting myself. I don't envy him."

"He runs a dog training business, but he's getting to the point where I think hiring an accountant would be a good idea. He's been doing too much on his own for the last couple of years, and it's time to get some additional help." Talking about Jackson had been a simple way to let them know about myself, but it also made it easier for me to relax.

Gregory nodded, understanding clear on his face. "That's the hard part. Your business gets to the point where you need either more hours in the day or more hands, and you have to figure out the best ways to delegate. I've seen a lot of people try to hold the reins too tightly for too long, and it negatively impacts the business."

"I can understand that. I think he sees there are better uses of his time than trying to do everything himself. It's just going to take some getting used to for him." Jackson was making good progress, though. It helped that putting us first was his main goal.

"It's one of those things you really have to consider." Gregory was now leaning against the table, clearly interested in the conversation. "When you don't sit down and figure out how much your time is actually worth, you can end up wasting your time on things that would be better served by having someone else do them."

Nodding, I relaxed back in the chair. "Absolutely, and I'm glad Jackson is starting to see that. I think if he was still single he'd be trying to do it all. Hopefully, getting him help will not only give him a better balance in his life but will also let him focus on growing the business."

"With a small business, growth is always important. If you're not careful, you'll turn around, and there will be more competition than you realized."

Deciding it was time to bring the conversation back to why we were actually there, I nodded again. "Is that why your new development is so far out of town? I was looking at it on the map earlier, and I was surprised at the location."

Gregory shrugged, but it wasn't a casual gesture. It was more of an agreement. "There are a lot of developments in the area that are nice and are a good value for buyers. However, they're almost identical copies of one another. I think we've reached a point where people are looking for something different. It will be a little bit of a drive, but I think when people see the amenities and lifestyle that being farther out can offer, they'll be intrigued."

"Are you referring to the fact that there would be space for a pool and gym, or are you referring to something else?" Having amenities in planned communities were becoming less frequent. We'd worked on one a few months ago, and their idea of a community pool had been no bigger than a hot tub.

Gregory continued as everyone else listened, so he didn't seem to have an issue discussing the new planned community. "We were able to get enough space that there will be room for a good-sized aquatic center and gym, but what I'd really like to see is walking trails and parks."

"Something like that would be very different than what people are finding out there right now. Really, the only community that currently boasts a walking trail is literally a big loop around the outside of the development." The plan had a lot of potential. "I think you've got a good idea."

Cooper and I hadn't been looking to buy a house but driving around, we'd noticed the different developments. I'd even driven through several of them to see what their landscaping was like, and I hadn't been impressed.

As the conversation continued, several of the managers joined in and even my boss. As long as the conversation stayed around community layouts and respective plans, they couldn't screw things up too badly.

With Gregory occupied, Chris turned to me, dropping his voice low. "I hope you didn't feel the need to out yourself at work over making us feel more comfortable."

"No, they're aware of Jackson." But it was nice of him to worry.

"Good, it was awkward enough at the beginning that I wasn't sure."

I had to chuckle. "No, they're not homophobic, just socially inept."

Chris smiled and nodded. "I can see that."

"I think it's more of a case of overthinking it than anything deliberate. You won't find anyone at the company who has an issue with your relationship." With a project that big, it had to be something they'd known could be an issue. There would be too many subcontractors and workers to keep all of it out.

"It's good to know." He looked down at the table then back at me, dropping his voice again. "I shouldn't be saying this, but some of your competition didn't make the best first impression."

I could only imagine. "At least it makes it clear you don't want to work with them."

To go to all the trouble of arranging for meetings and dinners to hopefully get a contract and lose it because some of your people were assholes would be terrible. It made my boss look a little bit better. He might be a moron, but his intentions weren't bad, and he was trying.

That didn't mean he was off the hook, though. No, he and I would have to talk about him springing things on me.

Picking up the menu, I started browsing through it as I got

to know Chris. He was interesting and funny. I'd spent most of the day obsessing over the dinner, and I was determined to enjoy it. I might have just been there to show the customers we were an inclusive organization, but that didn't mean I couldn't enjoy the food and the company.

I hoped Cooper and Jackson were having fun on their date. Knowing Cooper, they were having a great deal of it. Hopefully, they weren't completely worn out by the time I got home. I'd imagined arriving back at the house tired and grumpy, but a very different picture was starting to emerge.

3

JACKSON

PANCAKES AND SYRUP weren't the best way to calm my excited pup down, especially when he'd clearly had too much coffee as well. It was what he'd wanted on our date, though. By the time he'd gotten home from work, Cooper was bouncing off the walls. He'd grinned and changed the subject when I'd asked how much coffee he'd consumed. I just told him we were going to make rules on coffee consumption, especially on days we were going out for pancakes.

He'd pouted and snuggled up to me, trying to get me to forget what we'd been talking about. It'd almost worked. His conversations had been bouncing around just as much as his body, making me smile. "...and then we get to the end and she shrugs and says she's changed her mind—she doesn't really need all that sugar and just to give her a plain black coffee. I almost died. Who does that to somebody?"

"I can't imagine wanting that many things done to my coffee, and half the steps you listed didn't even sound like English." Coffee was really a foreign language sometimes.

Cooper laughed and shook his head before devouring a bite of pancake. After taking a sip of his milk, his chattering began again. "Still no word on the new building, I've heard they're getting closer. The gossip is that they're only days away from announcing it."

Cooper had volleyed between being excited and confident and nervous and unsure. He wanted the promotion, but he was afraid that with his schooling and everything we had going on around the house, there wouldn't be time.

I knew we needed to make a schedule and figure out the best way to make it work. My suggestion to cut back some of his hours of work had been met with caution. The idea was practical; he'd admitted that, but it was also stressful because he was worried it would make him look like he wasn't serious about the job.

He had a point, but there were only so many hours in the day.

"You would be a great manager, and I know they're going to see it." We'd had similar discussions for weeks, but I would keep repeating it until he was confident. Or at least so bored with the conversation that he decided believing me was easier.

Cooper nodded. "And if I don't get this one, I work toward my degree, and we figure out what else I need to do to stand out."

That was the other part of the discussion. I wanted him to believe in himself, but I also wanted him to see that it wouldn't be the end of the world if he didn't get it. There were a lot of things he could do to improve his chances.

"How did Lee work out today? Do you still have a lot of paperwork to do?" Cooper took another big bite of pancakes, and for a moment, I worried he would choke. But deep-throating skills came in handy when someone was as passionate about pancakes as Cooper was.

Trying not to grin, I focused on his question, glad to be able to tell him that my new employee was working out wonderfully. "Classes went great, and she's fitting right in.

Having another set of hands has been wonderful. She even agreed to stay late and get some of the billing done for me." It shouldn't have taken me as long as it had to realize I'd needed help. The guys had been right; doing everything myself was unreasonable.

Cooper beamed. "Told you so."

I laughed. "And you're going to keep reminding me about that until we're a hundred, aren't you?"

Cooper nodded, clearly pleased with being right. "Yes, I don't want you to forget. Oh, speaking of me being right, you said you were going to tell me what the surprise was."

I laughed. "One thing has nothing to do with the other, pup. No, I'm not going to fall for that."

Cooper blinked at me, giving me that perfectly innocent expression. "Of course it does. If I'm right about one thing, I'm right about the other."

Chuckling, I reached over and ran my hand over his head. "Are you trying to weasel an answer out of me, or are you just trying to be naughty enough that I'll give you a spanking when we get home?"

He honestly seemed to think about it.

I tried not to smile as he considered his options. He was so funny.

Finally, he shrugged. "Both. If I actually get an answer, that would be perfect. But it would be even *more* perfect to get a spanking. So you could just give me both. You tell me the answer, then say you have to punish me for being naughty enough to get the answer out of you." He beamed like he'd solved all the world's problems in one fell swoop. "See? That's an amazing idea."

Shaking my head, I didn't try to hide my smile. "Of course, it's perfect. But I thought you had something else in mind for when we got home."

Cooper shivered and licked his lips. His eyes got heated, and he leaned closer to me in the booth. "I'm sure you can find a way to do it all, Master."

"My sexy, naughty boy. What am I going to do with you?" It was a rhetorical question, but Cooper grinned.

"I can help you think of a long list if you need me to."

I was still laughing when our waitress came back over to the table. "How are you two doing? Goodness, you must have a hollow leg." She found the amount of food Cooper could consume startling.

Smiling, I shook my head. "I don't know where he puts it."

Cooper smiled at her and cut another piece. "It's because they're so fabulous. I love pancakes, and you guys make the best."

She smiled at him but shook her head disbelievingly. "Just don't eat so much you pop. Now, is there anything else I can do for you?"

As I declined, she laid the ticket on the table. "You two let me know if you change your mind. But I don't think he needs any dessert."

Her mothering instincts went off the charts when Cooper was around, but I didn't think to disagree with her. She was right.

She glanced across the table at the empty side of the booth. "You never did say where your other young man is."

"He had to work late." Being able to spend the evening with Cooper was nice, but it'd felt like something was missing. I wasn't sure how they saw it, but I was happiest when we were all together.

She nodded. "How about I pack up a slice of pie for him?"

Cooper nodded enthusiastically. "Oh, yes! He'd love that."

"Just for him, though. You've had entirely too much sugar and caffeine today." There was no negotiating on that.

Cooper gave me a little smile but nodded. "Just for Sawyer."

She laughed at us both and walked off, telling me she would leave the pie at the register. Cooper was nearly done with his pancakes, so I watched as he took a few more bites. It had been too much food for me to begin with, and I wasn't going to try to compete with him.

When it looked like he was finally full, I pushed my plate away and took one last sip of my water. "Are you ready to go?"

He sighed and looked over at the counter where the desserts were displayed. "I guess so."

Laughing, I ignored his not-so-subtle hint. "All right then, how much time do you think we have before he gets home? I meant to ask him this morning, but I forgot."

It had been what I'd initially gone to the kitchen for. Unfortunately, I hadn't remembered that until he was driving away. His worries and the need to comfort him had distracted me. I was hoping that the meeting had gone better than he'd feared.

Cooper dug into his pocket and checked his phone. "Another couple of hours probably, unless it goes terribly. He was so nervous this morning."

"It should be fine. We'd have heard from him by now if it had gone badly." That was the only thing that kept me from worrying too much.

Cooper nodded. "Yeah, he'd have called if it had gone badly, but I don't like seeing him that worked up. He's just always so calm, so it's hard when he's upset."

There was no arguing with that. Sawyer was always the one who projected a calm assurance that everything would work out, and seeing him so nervous hurt my heart. But on another level, it had made me feel good. He was finally starting to be comfortable showing us when he was worried. To me, it sounded like he knew he was safe enough to let go and not hide what was going on inside him.

Cooper leaned over and gave me a kiss on the cheek. "We'll

have dessert and distractions ready for him if he comes home in a bad mood."

Smiling, I moved my hand to rest on his leg and gave it a squeeze. "You're right. Okay, let's go. If we stay here any longer, you're going to think about getting another pancake."

I was slightly serious, but Cooper laughed. "Next time, I'm going to get the ones with the chocolate hazelnut spread and bananas. That looked good. Oh, or maybe the chocolate and strawberry ones."

Walking through the restaurant with Cooper was always an experience. He kept looking at people's plates and trying to decide what he wanted to eat next time. As we walked in, he'd been overwhelmed with the number of choices, and it had taken him forever to pick. "Either one would be delicious."

And enough sugar to kill a horse.

"Oh, I'll get one, and you can get the other, and then we'll be able to try them both."

I had a feeling he was going to end up eating both and leaving me with nothing. "We'll see."

Cooper seemed to take that to mean he could talk me into it and grinned. He was still so bouncy it didn't take long to get the bill paid and for us to leave. As we headed out of the restaurant and to the car, I was glad we'd been able to find a spot toward the side of the building.

The car was in the shadows on the other part of the lot from where most people were parked. As we got to it, I pulled Cooper into my arms and leaned against the hood. He gasped but pressed himself against me harder. "How have you liked your first date so far, baby?"

Cooper was so excited he almost vibrated energy, but he gave me a sweet, innocent look as he peered up at me. "It's been wonderful, but it's not over yet, is it?"

Shaking my head, I ran my hands slowly up and down his

back. "Not unless you wanted it to be. I thought you could come back to my place. How does that sound?"

His eyes got big, and he started nibbling on his bottom lip. Peering up at me, he gave me a cautious look. "But we wouldn't go too far, right? It's my first date, and I'm a good boy."

God, he did that too well.

"Of course not." I let my hand drift down to his lower back and rubbed just above the waist of his pants. "But it's your first date. Don't you want a goodnight kiss once we get alone?"

He radiated just enough sweet curiosity that it was sexy and cute at the same time. "You won't think I'm naughty if I say yes?"

Oh yes, Sawyer was right. Cooper should've been a porn star.

"No, baby, of course not. Because you saved that first kiss for me, didn't you?"

The little rascal even managed to blush. He nodded slowly and gave me an innocent look. "But I thought you'd never noticed me."

"Oh, I would have never been able to ignore you." And wasn't that the truth?

He beamed like I hung the moon, but the flash of desire in his eyes gave him away. "Then yes, take me back to your house, please."

I let my hand slide down over his ass. "I want you to remember, baby. No matter what we do, I know you saved yourself for me."

A shiver ran through my wicked pup, and he nodded. I felt the tension in his body, and I knew how hard he was working not to grind his cock against me. Cooper was ready to race toward his orgasm, but I was going to make him wait.

Pushing him as close to the edge as I could without letting him go over was one of my favorite things, so no matter how much he wanted it, I wasn't going to rush his pleasure. I gave his ass a pat and moved my hands back up his body. "All right, baby, let's get you in the car."

The pat had another shiver running through Cooper, but he nodded. "Yes, Sir."

Letting him move away from me, I led him alongside the car and opened the passenger door for him. The drive home was longer than ever, but we filled the time with teasing flirting and the fun fantasy of his "first date."

As we parked and headed in, the need that had cooled began to heat back up. Cooper held my hand sweetly and kept giving me these innocent looks that made me want to completely corrupt him. Sawyer should have been there to see it, but I knew Cooper was going to have fun showing him how sexy he was later.

Opening the door, I led him in. "Would you like a tour?"

I closed the door and pulled him to me. "Or would you like to just cuddle on the couch? I think my baby needs his first kiss."

I was going to cover every inch of my sexy boy in kisses.

Cooper squeezed my hand and nodded, shy and slow. "Yes, I'd like to cuddle with you."

Taking him through the house, I brought him to the living room. I pulled him onto my lap as I sat down. We might have been playing that he was sweet and innocent, but I wasn't going to lose a chance to have him on my lap and wrapped in my arms.

"Oh, am I going to get my kiss now?" The too-innocent question had my cock jerking in my pants.

"Do you want your kiss, baby?"

He nodded slowly and leaned in closer. "Yes."

I cupped his cheek with one hand and wrapped my arm around him with the other. Bringing his face to mine, I gave him a tender kiss. But once the need was unleashed, it didn't stay sweet for long. When his mouth opened and my tongue flicked against his, Cooper moaned and started grinding himself against me.

The desire that poured off Cooper had my own need rising higher. He seemed to take every emotion and magnify it. Love or arousal, everything he was given exploded and expanded into something incredible.

The kiss kept pushing us higher. Cooper moaned low and made desperate sounds into my mouth. When he finally pulled away, it was to beg for more. "Please…more…"

Taking his mouth again, hotter and deeper, I let my hands move down to cup his ass. Palming his cheeks, I rocked his body against mine as we kissed. Cooper shivered and even through the layers of clothes, I could feel his straining erection.

The dominant part of me that had grown more vocal since I'd met my boys wanted to pull back and remind him that he couldn't come, but that would have ruined the moment. My excitable pup knew the rules, but he liked getting punished a little too much.

Cooper made desperate sounds and ground himself against me every time I pulled him closer. Finally at his breaking point, Cooper pulled away, breathing heavy with a sexy, just-kissed expression, and he gave me an innocent, "Come fuck me" look.

It was all Cooper and so perfect….I wanted to take him right there.

"I heard you can give kisses all over." He leaned in slowly and kissed my cheek. "Is that true?"

Trying not to show the wicked grin that wanted to escape, I nodded and wrapped my arms around him. Kissing down his neck, I paused long enough to whisper in his ear. "Do you want me to show you all the places I can kiss you, baby?"

Before he could nod, I had his shirt over his head and had started working my way down his neck again. Little breathy moans escaped as he sighed and pressed himself tighter against me. When I finally reached his chest and began kissing down his lean body, I flicked one nipple and smiled as he gasped.

"Do you want more kisses? I think you'll like all the places I can kiss and lick, baby." There was no doubt what Cooper wanted; sweet with feigned innocence or just with his normal excitement, my boy was frantic for more.

Going back and forth between his sensitive nubs, I alternated between light licks and teasing nibbles. The tender caresses made him whine, and the gentle bites made him moan and beg for more. When he was writhing and trying to get his cock closer to my body again, I wrapped my arms around him and turned us, so he was lying on the couch and I was stretched out over him.

"Do you want more kisses, baby?" I made my way down his chest and he nodded frantically.

His breathing was heavy, and anticipation seemed to send shivers through his body as I licked around his belly button and then moved even lower. "Are you sure? I'm going to kiss my boy all over."

Cooper's only response was to moan and try to thrust his hips up, though I had him pinned down to the couch. I unbuttoned his jeans and carefully eased the zipper over his hard cock as I chuckled. Shoving them down just enough to free him, I hovered over his erection and looked up at him.

"Do you want kisses here, baby?" Cooper's cock jerked and precum pearled at the slit. Another shiver ran through him and he nodded.

"Please...yes...please..." The rambling words were cut off as he moaned again when I pressed a kiss to the head of his length.

When I started licking and kissing down the shaft, he was a mess of pleading sounds and gasps of pleasure. I teased along his erection several times before I finally took him in my mouth.

He couldn't seem to decide if he was relieved the wait was over or desperate for more.

Going down on him, I took him as deep as I could and did my best to push him right to the edge. When he was begging for more and I could feel his body stiffen even harder, I moved off his cock and began to kiss down further.

His pants needed to go.

Sitting up, I tugged at his pants, and in seconds, I had my boy naked and splayed open for me. Cooper didn't try to hide what he wanted; his body wouldn't let him. I lay back down between his legs, and I pinned them up to his chest and kept him open for me. Kissing and licking at his balls, it wasn't long before I inched lower.

"I'm going to show you the most intimate kiss of all, baby." Cooper gasped and tried to thrust his body closer as I flicked my tongue over his tight hole.

Chuckling low, I kept up the slow, tender pace and teased circles around the ring of muscle before finally letting my tongue slide into his body. Cooper cried out and shook as I kissed and made love to him with my mouth. When I reached up and started slowly jerking him off, I thought he would come in seconds, but he did his best to hold back and be good for me. It had to be driving him crazy, but it was beautiful.

He reached a point where it was all too much. My sweet boy began begging frantically. "Please…make love to me… please…I need…"

Giving his body one last lick, I sat up. If he wanted me to make love to him, then there were a few things we needed.

Before I could finish sitting up, lube magically appeared next to us, making me jump and Cooper sigh with pleasure.

4

COOPER

"I love you so much, Sawyer." He had the best timing.

Sawyer grinned and shook his head as he kneeled down by the couch. Giving me a kiss while Jackson stripped, his free hand reached out and started teasing around my nipples, keeping the pleasure flowing through me. "Did you have a good time with Master?"

"I was his curious virgin, and he gave me my first kiss." Sawyer's smile widened, and I sighed. Master was loving and tender and taking his sweet time getting naked.

I could have been done in seconds, but it was taking him forever. Sawyer gave me another quick kiss. "I bet you were a wicked virgin."

Smirking, I shook my head, completely lying. "I was sweet and sexy and loved my first kiss...all of them. Master was showing me *all* the places he could kiss me."

Sawyer must have liked that idea, because his head came down over my chest and he kissed and trailed his tongue down my body, licking and tasting. Desire started building again, and my eyes closed as he got closer and closer to my cock.

They were both trying to drive me crazy.

When his mouth finally licked around the head of my dick, I felt Jackson's finger circle my hole. It was perfect and almost too much pleasure. I kept telling myself I wasn't going to come until Master gave me permission, but it was turning into an almost impossible promise.

One finger slowly entered me, and I almost flew off the couch. The press of their bodies against mine was the only thing that kept me grounded to the couch. All I could do was moan and writhe in protest as they slowly tortured me.

Sawyer kept his kisses light and almost teasing, and Jackson seemed to be in no hurry to stretch me. "No more teasing. You have to fuck me."

Shit.

Jackson's finger slid deep to caress my prostate, making it hard to concentrate. "My sweet pup needs to be punished. He forgot how to be good."

Sawyer's head came up, and he made a low sound like he was disappointed, but a wicked pleasure surged through me. "I'm sorry, Master."

"Master's giving you pleasure, and you get demanding and needy. He's going to have to punish you, Cooper." Sawyer's words were husky and devilish, but they came out almost reasonable, like Master had no choice but to show me what a naughty boy I'd been.

So. Fucking. Hot.

I forced open my eyes as I shook, fireworks shooting off in me with every pass of Jackson's finger over the bundle of nerves. "I'm sorry, Master."

It might have sounded more believable if I'd been less needy —and if I could have made my body stay still.

Every gentle stroke made it more impossible, and my hips kept jerking on their own. Jackson pulled his finger almost all the way out before lining up a second finger and sinking it in slowly. His naked body kneeling on the couch, staring down at me with desire shining from his eyes, made it harder to rein in the passion that was starting to build.

The strong muscles begged to be touched, and the hard cock that jutted up from his groin begged to be licked. His sexy voice didn't help my situation any either. "You were very naughty, weren't you? I bet you want me to show you how to be a good boy for me."

Fuck.

His two thick fingers sent waves of pleasure through me, and the stretch was almost perfect...but I needed more. "Yes, I'm sorry. Show me how to be good."

I'd have promised him anything if I could have gotten to come—but whatever the punishment was—I desperately wanted it.

"That's right. I'll show you how to behave." His low, understanding voice made it even more erotic. It sounded so rational, but it was going to be beautifully wicked.

When he pulled the two fingers out and slid in a third, I almost pleaded again. But Sawyer's mouth on my dick kept the words strangled in my throat. As they both pulled away, a desperate moan escaped, and I squeezed my eyes shut, trying to hold back every word and twitch that could get me in even more trouble. I wanted enough to be punished but not enough to push things so far I didn't get to come.

That wouldn't have been any fun.

At least, not right then. Another time the denial would have been perfect, but I'd been teased and pushed too far. I needed to come.

When I heard the sound of the condom wrapper, relief flooded through me. I felt the couch shift as Jackson looked at my face and chuckled. Sawyer's mouth moved away, but his hand took its place, keeping up the same teasing slow pleasure.

Jackson stretched out over me, and I finally looked up into

his eyes. Love and desire and happiness seemed to pour out of him. He leaned down and gave me a tender kiss before glancing over and doing the same to Sawyer. "My sweet boys. I love you."

Sawyer gave Jackson a quiet response, but my words were trapped in my throat as Jackson sank deep into me in one thrust. Once I found my voice, I cried out as he made love to me. He'd go slowly before speeding up and pounding at me to push me right to the edge. I could almost feel my orgasm crashing over me, but then he'd switch it up to a deliberately unhurried pace.

Sawyer watched with a smile on his face and matched Jackson's rhythm just to torture me. I'd lost track of how long they made love to me and how many rounds of the maddening cycles they'd done, but eventually, I got to the point where the slow tender lovemaking was going to make me come.

Low whines escaped and I couldn't hold back the pleading any longer. "Please let me come...Master...please...Sawyer faster please..."

They both chuckled, and it was a low, wicked sound that sent another shiver through me. "But I love seeing you right on the edge, pup. I love watching the need build inside you."

"Love seeing me come too...please?" Jackson seemed to thoroughly enjoy driving me insane.

If it had stayed slow and deliberate, it might have been enough to send me into subspace, but the way he kept switching it up made it impossible to let go. It was incredible, but I was ready to lose my mind—or just shove Sawyer's hand out of the way and make myself come.

"Please...please...please..." I didn't realize I was begging until Jackson took my mouth in a heated kiss and stopped the flood of words.

As he fucked me harder, I alternated between wanting to chase the pleasure and trying to hold it back....I didn't know what to do. But Jackson seemed ready to decide for me. He tilted my hips, so every thrust was hitting my prostate. Suddenly, Sawyer's hand tightened almost painfully, and it was too perfect.

"Come." The rough order...the strong grip...the perfection of Jackson's cock fucking me...it all combined as my orgasm exploded through me. I could feel cum shooting out onto Sawyer's hand and Jackson's jerky thrusts as he gave in and let his own orgasm flood through him.

When the pleasure was finally fading, and I was lying on the couch completely spent, Jackson gave me a tender kiss and pulled out of me. As he moved away from the couch to deal with the condom, Sawyer scooted even closer and seemed to wrap himself around me.

I yawned and cuddled into him, wanting to hold him—but not in any hurry to move. "We don't need that...and I can do it...right?"

Sawyer laughed and sat up to look at me. Shaking his head, he gave me a quick kiss. "That didn't make any sense at all."

Yes it did...didn't it?

Maybe I'd left some parts out.

"Do you think we still need condoms?" Giving Sawyer a wicked but sleepy grin, I reached out and traced one finger over his chest until I found his nipples. "Think of how good it would feel to have him marking you like that."

Sawyer gave a low moan, and a shiver raced through him. Yep, he was steady and loving and had an imagination as dirty as mine. "Why don't we ask Master what he thinks?"

"Ask Master about what, naughty pup?" Jackson's teasing words had us both looking toward the hall where he'd come back from the bathroom.

Sawyer seemed nervous, but I thought the idea was too hot not to mention. If he wasn't ready that was fine, but I needed him to know what I wanted.

He was Master.

"Not using condoms anymore."

Jackson smiled as he walked over. The washcloth in his hand was warm as he cleaned the cum off my stomach and Sawyer's hand. He was clearly thinking it over, but Jackson did that about most things. He didn't just jump into a decision where he might regret it later. He thought it out. He might not need a long time, but when he made a decision, I never had to worry about it.

"As long as Sawyer is comfortable with it, then I say we get tested this week." Jackson set the washcloth on the floor and wrapped his arms around Sawyer. "What do you think?"

Sawyer curled into him, and I could see the stress of the day melt away with just that one touch. He nodded and glanced at me. I smiled. "He likes the idea. He thinks it's hot."

Jackson laughed and kissed the top of Sawyer's head. "Is that right? I bet Cooper has some naughty fantasies....What about you?"

Sawyer sighed and nodded. He might not always be comfortable talking about his fantasies, but he wouldn't hide something like that from Master. "Yes...I like the idea...and he's right."

"I'm always right." I was beginning to get a second wind, but as I sat up, I still felt sticky. "I'm also in need of a shower."

Jackson chuckled, but his hands rubbed along Sawyer's back and legs, and I knew he thought it was a good idea too. He nodded and gave me a thorough look. "I think you both need a shower. Sawyer has had a long day, and you seem to be still covered in cum, even though I just wiped you down."

He was shaking his head like I'd somehow made a mess on purpose, so I grinned and shrugged. Sawyer laughed and nodded. "Sounds good."

Jackson helped us both to stand and herded us toward the bathroom. I got kisses and hugs and a smack on the ass when I waved my butt at him. Sawyer got hugs and kisses and questions as Jackson turned on the water. "How was dinner?"

"Surprising, but not as bad as I was expecting." Slowly stripping off his clothes, Sawyer's answer wasn't as information-filled as Jackson and I were clearly hoping.

"What's that mean?" With his hands trapped in his shirt, I reached out and tickled down his ribs, so I could see him squirm.

"Stop that, Coop." Sawyer laughed and wiggled while Jackson chuckled.

"Then tell us more." That was the only way I was going to leave him alone. He had a tendency to bottle things up, and it was up to me to make sure I poked him enough to get it out.

He chuckled and gave me a look like I was a kid he was humoring. As he kept taking off his clothes, he finally started giving real information. "Well, the actual dinner was good. I liked the restaurant, but it was kind of awkward."

He paused for a moment to take off his socks. But before I could prod him for more details, he kept going. "The owners are a gay guy and his partner. My boss is evidently a moron and wanted to make sure there was someone at the table they could relate to. Don't get me wrong—I had a nice time talking to both of them, but that seemed to be the only reason I was invited."

Sawyer shook his head at the memory and leaned into Jackson's touch as he came up behind Sawyer and gave him a hug. "It was probably a good idea, though. In trying not to do anything offensive, they looked uncomfortable and stiff. They would have come across as homophobic. The owner's husband said they had dinner with one of the other firms in town recently, and they said some truly asshole comments. I think we've got a good shot. Once everyone relaxed, the dinner went well."

Jackson chuckled. "So even though it was a ridiculous reason to want you there, it turned out to be the right choice?"

"Yes. It's hard to be angry about that. On one hand, they all need to relax and should have treated them like any other couple, but on the other, it's a step in the right direction that they realized they needed help. I still think being frustrated about it is reasonable, but I liked the guys, so I don't know."

"Other than some occasionally weird questions, the picnic went good, so I'm not sure why the dinner would have been different. Well, okay, I can see why your boss was worried. He's starting to realize he's a moron. Everyone else should have been functional." They hadn't been *that* bad at the picnic.

Sawyer sighed. "I think it was mostly about worrying that he would offend someone. They really want the contract. It would be a huge financial boost this year, and that makes some people worry too much. I think if so much hadn't been on the line it wouldn't have been an issue. By the time the food arrived at the table, it was fine, but their caution about accidentally offending them would have easily looked like they had an issue with their relationship."

He really was surrounded by morons at work.

I loved that he'd found a job he liked but some days, I just wished he had more actual adults at his company. Leaning in, I kissed him quickly. "At least you were there to keep it from going to shit. Hopefully, that will help you when you're up for a raise or promotion."

Sawyer smiled and nodded. Before he could say anything, Jackson started moving us to the shower. "Come on, you two. We're going to run out of hot water."

It was a tight fit, but we made it work. Jackson and I had already come, so we spent the time lazily focusing on Sawyer. We weren't in any hurry, but we were enjoying touching him and helping him relax. By the time we were clean, Sawyer was hard, and no longer thinking about work. No…his mind was on other things.

Jackson slowly dried off Sawyer while I quickly wiped

down and bounced around the bathroom, finishing getting ready for bed. I couldn't decide if I was exhausted or finding my second wind, but curling up with them on the bed sounded perfect.

Kissing down Sawyer's neck, Jackson was in a completely different headspace. He wanted to make sure Sawyer was just as worn out as he'd made me. Watching the way his hands dragged the towel over Sawyer's skin was making my cock thicken—which was why I tried to stay out of the way.

It was Sawyer's turn for attention.

When Jackson wrapped his arms around Sawyer and pressed his cock to Sawyer's ass so he could reach around and dry Sawyer's cock, my mouth watered. God, they were so sexy together. I'd never get over how beautiful they were when they pressed close and kissed.

With me, Jackson was playful and willing to explore anything that caught my eye or my dick, but with Sawyer, he was tender and loving until that point where Sawyer was begging to be taken. They were perfect together and perfect for me....I'd always known we'd find the right person to complete our family, but Jackson was more incredible than I'd ever imagined.

By the time Sawyer was *thoroughly* dried, I was leaning against the counter, watching my two men. Eventually, Jackson pulled away giving Sawyer one last lingering kiss to his neck and put up the towels. "Go finish getting ready."

Sawyer shivered, making me smile. He shook his head at me and headed for the sink. Jackson gave me a questioning look. "Weren't you going to get ready for bed?"

Ready?

Oh, yes. "I got distracted."

Jackson chuckled and smiled at me like I was so cute he wanted to gobble me up. "Hurry, pup."

Giving him a cheeky grin, I turned back to the sink and reached for my toothbrush. "Yes, Master."

That earned a laugh from Sawyer and a smack on my ass from Jackson. Sighing, I wiggled my butt, trying for another one as I started brushing. Jackson snorted. "I'm not going to reward sass...not this time, at least."

Giggling, I tried to focus on what I was doing, but his lingering touches and the look in his eyes as he watched us made it difficult. Sawyer was in worse shape than I was, though. He was still hard, and his gaze kept following Jackson in the mirror.

When we were done, and it was Jackson's turn to use the sink, he pulled us both close and let his hands start wandering down to caress our asses. To me, the touch felt soothing and made me want to curl into him, but judging by the way Sawyer's body moved against Jackson's hip, he wasn't feeling relaxed at all.

With smacks to our asses and a couple of kisses, we were headed back into the bedroom. Sawyer and I climbed onto the bed and I wrapped my arms around him, making sure he was in the middle. He sighed and pressed closer, his cock hard and thick once again.

I frowned when I yawned. "I'm not that tired."

He laughed. "Bullshit. You even stopped bouncing around the bathroom and were leaning against the counter."

"You guys were just so cute, I had to watch." That was true but maybe not the complete truth, because I yawned again.

Sawyer grinned, and his hands caressed my chest slowly. "How did your date go?"

Closing my eyes, I smiled and hugged him tighter. "It was wonderful. The pancakes were great." Then I remembered the dessert. "Oh, we got you dessert. It's in the fridge."

We talked about other parts of the day and little random things like what we needed to get at the store. I was too comfortable to do anything drastic like open my eyes or roll over, so I let my hands wander down Sawyer's back and over his ass before moving up again.

By the time Jackson joined us, the words were taking longer to get from my head to my mouth. Sawyer pressed a kiss to my lips before rolling over to Jackson. I smiled as I pictured them curled up with Jackson's wandering hands working Sawyer's desire back up to a feverish pitch.

As everything got heavier, I sank into the pillows and let sleep pull me under. The last thing I remembered was soft whispered words and Sawyer's low laughter at something Jackson said. Knowing that he'd take care of Sawyer, I relaxed until everything faded away.

5

SAWYER

"EWW, that's gross. Is that what you do when I leave you alone?" Cooper looked a little green, and I was laughing so hard that I almost fell off the couch. Jackson's strong hold was the only thing that kept me from tumbling to the floor.

"It's not that bad, Cooper. I think you'd like some of it if you gave it another chance." Jackson was chuckling but still trying to take Cooper seriously.

It was just so difficult, though.

We'd lounged around all morning, relaxing and not really getting anything done. Unfortunately, Cooper eventually had to go to work, so we'd started functioning. Well, he had. Jackson and I'd just moved from the table to the couch. We were out of bed and had breakfast, so I thought we'd done pretty good. Not as fabulous as Cooper, who'd gotten ready for work, but it was my day to relax.

"It's raw fish and seaweed. That's all I need to say. Leaving you two alone is clearly dangerous." Cooper walked over and flopped down on the couch, stretching out over us. He looked up, his head on Jackson's lap, and puckered his lips.

Jackson grinned, leaned down, and kissed him. Of course,

Cooper looked at me expectantly as Jackson sat up. I laughed and stretched out, and my lips touched his tenderly. Sitting up, I ran my hands over his legs, and Jackson began playing with his hair. The little attention whore just snuggled closer and smiled.

"Just promise me you'll brush your teeth before I come home. It's too gross to even think about." The little drama queen was hamming it up, clearly not ready to go to work.

"We promise." Jackson gave in entirely too easily, but I snorted and shook my head.

"Are you going to bring me back dessert?" Cooper looked at me and batted his eyelashes. "Something good?"

"Of course." Jackson leaned down and kissed him again.

I reached out and tickled him. "You're trying to manipulate him."

Cooper wiggled and laughed, not attempting to pull away. He was enjoying the attention. Jackson chuckled and tightened his grip on Cooper, so the wiggly flirt wouldn't fall off the couch.

"It's not trying if it's working." Jackson sat up and smiled indulgently. "But I'll get him back later. He's got a punishment coming."

Giggling, Cooper tried to look guiltless and sweet as I relaxed my teasing fingers, but he was having too much fun to pull it off. "What kind of punishment?"

Jackson shook his head, still smiling. "I'm not going to tell you. I'm going to let you think about it all day at work."

Cooper gave Jackson a pretty pout that made both of us look at him with a hungry expression. The little tease. "But that's so mean."

"And you're such a little manipulator." Laughing, I started tickling him again.

Jackson chuckled as Cooper squealed and wiggled in our arms. By the time I stopped tickling him and was simply caressing him softly, he was out of breath and looked almost like he was ready for subspace. Part need, part desire, he looked as if all he wanted was to stretch out and let us have our way with him.

My cock loved the idea, but there just wasn't time. Jackson leaned down and pressed another kiss to Cooper's mouth. His low words sent a shiver through us both. "So tempting. But you have to go to work."

That wasn't what he'd wanted to hear, but he didn't pout for long. "But when I get home?"

Jackson turned to focus his heated gaze on me. "When you get home, we already have plans with Sawyer. Don't we?"

"Oh yes, that's right." Cooper sat up and wiggled until he was straddled across my lap. He leaned in and gave me a smacky kiss. "We're going to have so much fun tonight."

I couldn't decide if I needed to be worried or not.

"That always sounds a little dangerous coming from you." Cooper gave me a sexy pout as I teased him.

Jackson nodded and grinned at Cooper's drama. "Something about that innocent face and the wicked things that you know lie right under the surface."

Cooper's lip came out even further, but his eyes were laughing. "I'm just not appreciated."

Not falling for it, I laughed and pulled him closer to give him a kiss, nibbling on that sexy lip of his. "It's because we know you too well." As he pulled away smiling, I couldn't resist giving him a hug. "I love you."

"I love you too. Have fun today with Master." The low, whispered words curled right through me.

Before I could respond, he moved away and leaned over to give Jackson a kiss. As he climbed off my lap, bouncing excitedly again, he started patting himself down. "Keys, phone...what am I missing?"

"Common sense...humility..." I couldn't resist.

Cooper looked like he was ready to dive back onto the couch and show me that I would regret my teasing comments, but Jackson pulled me into his arms.

"No more. Don't make him late." As I tumbled onto his lap, I felt his hand smack my ass, and I moaned.

Cooper vibrated with excitement. "Oh, yes, he needs a spanking, Master." Then he gave Jackson a hopeful look. "But wait until I get home, please?"

Jackson nodded. "But it's not going to get you out of being punished."

Cooper shivered. "I want to be punished too."

"My naughty boys." Jackson's tender tone was at odds with the words, but it sent the heat level in the room skyrocketing. "Okay, tease, time for work, or you'll be late. Drive safely."

Cooper nodded and came closer to give us both quick kisses before he headed for the door. "Don't forget my dessert."

Laughing, I called out after him. "Do you really want dessert from a sushi restaurant? It could get interesting."

I couldn't see his face as he hollered back, but the disgust in his voice was real. "Gross. You'd better not bring me a dead fish dessert."

As the door slammed behind him, Jackson was still chuckling. "What do you think he was picturing?"

"I don't even want to know." Cooper's imagination could be a frightening place.

Turning around in Jackson's lap to get more comfortable, I curled into him and let my head relax on his shoulder. "I'm not sure the sushi restaurant even has dessert."

Jackson chuckled as he wrapped his arms around me and relaxed against the couch. "We'll stop somewhere on the way back and get him something."

"Just him?"

"No, we'll get something for everyone." Then suddenly Jackson grinned and looked as if a lightbulb should have gone off over his head. "But if you'd like, we could make something here."

"Like bake something?" I wasn't sure that was such a good idea. We'd managed to make a box cake mix taste funny. Not to mention the texture.

Jackson heard the disbelief in my words, and from the sound in his voice, I knew he was trying not to laugh. "Yes. We could make brownies or maybe a cheesecake. We need to go to the grocery store later anyway."

I liked the idea of cooking with Jackson, but it seemed complicated. "Have you ever made a cheesecake?"

"Yes. It's not as hard as it seems. I promise. I think it would be fun, but I want today to be about doing things with you. So if it doesn't sound good, then we'll pick something up at the bakery later to surprise him with." Jackson's gentle caress was making it hard to remember why it had seemed like an iffy idea to begin with.

"We killed a box cake mix, and you don't want to know what Cooper did to a pan of brownies, so you've got to be in charge of it." Some people would have thought I was kidding, but Jackson knew to take me seriously.

"But you'll help?" The hand that had been slowly stroking my arm moved to my leg, and I couldn't decide if it was making me relaxed or turned on. My brain and my dick couldn't quite make up their minds.

"Yes." He was a patient teacher in the kitchen and seemed to enjoy showing us things that he thought were fun or important. "When do you want to go to the store?"

"How about we get some breakfast and another cup of coffee and then figure that out?" He pressed a kiss to the side of my head, making me smile. "I thought you might like to have time as a pup today."

The words were still sweet and tender, but I could hear a nervousness in them that I hadn't felt from Jackson since the beginning. It took me a second to figure out why he was cautious — Cooper had always been there too, when I'd been a pup.

Nothing about the idea seemed wrong or made me nervous. It was something I'd always done with Cooper. Even though we were very different kinds of pups, I'd never thought about doing it alone. But with Jackson, I wouldn't be alone.

"I'd like that. Maybe while you watch a movie or something, so you won't get bored?" Curling up with me was very different from throwing the ball around for Cooper. He needed the attention and action, and all I wanted was to be cuddled and loved on while I relaxed.

"That sounds like a perfect way to spend the afternoon."

Jackson brought one hand up and caressed my face and hair. "So how about this? Coffee and breakfast, and then we'll get ready for the day and go to the grocery store. When we get back, we can get you ready and cuddle for a while."

"That works, but the idea of getting up sucks. I like lying here with you."

I could hear the grin in his voice. "I can tempt you with coffee and pie for breakfast as long as you don't pull a Cooper and bounce off the walls for the rest of the day."

Smiling, I decided to play hard to get. "Hmm, that bribe might work, but I think you can make it even sweeter."

Jackson pretended to think about it, making all kinds of silly thinking sounds. "How about I help you get a shower and wash you *thoroughly* before we go?"

Perfect. But I'd learned from the best. "Am I going to get to come after you *thoroughly* wash me?"

Jackson burst out laughing. "Are you channeling Cooper?"

"Yes." Straightening, I gave him a suspicious look. "And you didn't answer my question."

He gave me a teasing look. "I'm not going to promise you an orgasm, but I will promise to wash *every* inch of you."

He was sexy and perfect and clearly learning too well how to tempt me. "Okay, but I have a feeling you're going to keep me hard and crazy all day."

He gave me an innocent look *almost* worthy of Cooper. "Would I do that?"

"Yes."

"What would be better…to be teased and washed and have to stay hard or to be locked away so you can't get hard to begin with?" His wicked words went straight to my dick.

It was an impossibly hard decision. "That's not fair."

Chuckling, he gave me a quick kiss and pat on my hip. "Breakfast."

Doing my best Cooper impression, I batted my eyelashes and gave him a pout. "Yes, Master."

As I stood, his hands caressed down my sides and his thumbs stretched out to tease around my dick. "I think that a spanking for you would be a good idea later."

Was that supposed to be a punishment?

Even if I could have gotten the words out, begging for it seemed like a bad idea just in case it was. There were other easier ways I could get my point across, though. As Jackson stood, I pressed myself closer to him and started running my hands up his chest. "Whatever you think, Master."

His chuckle was wicked and low and sent shivers down my spine right to my dick. "That's my good boy."

Did good boys get to come?

"But breakfast first. Come on." He pressed a kiss to my forehead as I stepped away.

"What kind of pie did you get me?"

He wrapped one arm around me but stopped to think for a moment. "I have no idea. Cooper was the one who looked, and the waitress said she was going to pack something up for you since we were mean and came without you."

"She said that?"

Jackson shrugged but smiled. "She implied it. She asked about you right away."

"That's cute." I was glad that they'd had a chance to do something together, but it was wonderful she'd accepted us so easily. Some people would always be surprised—we got crazy looks in the grocery store—but it was nice that it wasn't that shocking to everyone.

As we made our way into the kitchen, my mind started shifting from cuddling and flirting with Jackson to actual things that needed to be accomplished. "Should we make a grocery list when we go so we can get stuff for the week?"

We'd been talking about doing another grocery trip for a couple of days, but we hadn't found the right time for us all to go. Sending one person with a list would have been the most practical decision, but that wasn't as much fun. But it also seemed to keep us from forgetting things as easily, so there was a good reason for it too.

Jackson glanced over to the fridge. "Probably, but let's do a bigger trip tomorrow. We'll grab a few things we know we need just in case, but we'll do the rest with Cooper."

"Sounds good." Heading over to the coffee, I saw it was almost empty, so I started making a new pot. As I moved around the kitchen, I glanced at Jackson. "Was there anything else we had to do this weekend?"

Jackson had made sure to have time off between the most recent sessions of his weekend groups, and I knew we needed to use the time wisely and not goof off. Jackson shook his head and walked over to the counter while I finished getting the coffee going.

I thought he was going to reach for a cup in the cabinet over my head, but he pinned me to the counter and began kissing down my neck. "This weekend is going to be as little work as possible, even stuff around the house. I want you to relax. You spent too much time last week tense and stressed out."

He was right, but that didn't mean we needed to get nothing done this weekend. "But—"

Jackson nipped my neck cutting off what I was going to say and making me moan. "No, you don't get to be reasonable. With three adults, and Cooper's and my odd schedules, there's enough time during the week to get things done if we need to."

I wanted to argue to see if he would do it again, but I just nodded. "You're right."

Jackson's low chuckle sent a shiver down my spine. "I'm glad you see it my way. But how should you have said that statement?"

He was going to make me crazy. "You're right, Master."

He made a low pleasured sound and licked up the side of my neck. "That's right, but I think I'm going to have to spend the day reminding you of that."

The moan that broke out was impossible to hold back. I hoped that *crazy* wouldn't end up being an understatement.

6

JACKSON

BAKING WASN'T SUPPOSED to be that sexy. But everything with my boys was more perfect and more erotic. With Cooper and his exuberance out of the mix, making the cheesecake with Sawyer had taken on a tender turn, one with lingering touches and me finding any excuse to wrap my arms around him.

"It's going to be wonderful. You did a great job." Giving him a kiss, I dragged Sawyer out of the kitchen, where he'd been staring at the stove with a skeptical expression on his face.

"But it looked runny...are you sure?" Sawyer gave the stove one last look as I dragged him out.

"It's supposed to look like that. It gets more solid as it cooks. I promise." I tried not to smile, but he was so cute.

"I don't know. It looks like pudding with too much milk in it. That stuff never sets if you don't follow the directions. Just ask Cooper." He said it so seriously, I knew there had to be a good story.

I gave up trying not to laugh. "Come on. It's going to take a while, and I promise it will turn out fine."

Asking what Cooper had done to the pudding was probably not the best idea at that point, but it had to have been fabulous.

Sawyer nodded, but I knew his mind was still back there in the kitchen, second-guessing the dessert.

My sweet worrier.

He wouldn't have been thinking of it for himself. No, his concern was probably about wanting it to turn out perfect for Cooper or wanting to make me proud of him. Stopping and taking his hand, I pulled him close and wrapped my arms around him. "I love spending time with you. You know that? Even if it turns to goo and is completely inedible, I had fun because we did it together."

Sawyer's face was pressed into my neck, and I felt him nod. He'd had such a long week. Even without the issues at work, he'd been stressed. He wanted Cooper to get the promotion more than Cooper did, and he worried about the classes and school in general.

It was time for him to let it all go.

"We're going to get you ready, and you're going to relax for a while. I'm going to cuddle with my pup while I watch a movie, and we're not going to think about anything. How does that sound?" Sawyer sighed, and I felt his breath tickle my skin. The sensation had me pulling him even closer.

"Good." The tone of his voice said the idea was more than simply good.

Wanting to lighten the mood, I huffed. "Just good?"

I could hear a smile in his voice. "Nice?"

Snorting, I shook my head. "I think that's worse than good."

He nearly giggled. "Pleasant?"

I groaned.

"Enjoyable?"

Laughing, I tightened my grip and wiggled my fingers like I was going to tickle him. Sawyer was doing his best not to laugh as he squirmed in my arms. "Okay, how about lovely?"

When all I did was snort, he tried again. "Gratifying?"

Teasing him a little, I gave him a heated look. "I'll show you gratifying if you want, but normally that's what Cooper wants, not you, my cuddly pup."

Sawyer pushed closer to me, and I could see a blush creeping up his face. Mumbling with a smile still in his voice, he was a little hard to understand. "How about we do the gratifying part later?"

Kissing his head, I smiled. "Whatever my pup needs."

He cuddled for a few more seconds before he pulled back and took my hand. He walked beside me as we went back to the bedroom, the anticipation building. We both knew what we wanted, so it didn't take long before we had his tail, collar, and mitts out on the floor. As I undressed him, Sawyer started to relax. By the time he was naked, the stress of the regular world had faded.

I pulled him into my arms and tucked him close against my body. His head went down on my shoulder again, and he sighed. I let him stand there as I caressed his back. It could have easily turned sexual, but it was about more than that. He needed a chance to let it all go and everything else to be nothing but background noise.

When his muscles loosened, I turned my head and gave him a kiss on the cheek. "Kneel for me. I'm going to finish getting you ready."

Even though it hadn't technically been that long since he'd been a pup, I knew it was something he needed more frequently. Just like most people needed to be able to unwind on a regular basis, so did Cooper and Sawyer. I knew I was going to have to look at the calendar and figure out a way to make sure he got that time.

When he was on all fours, I sat down beside him. There was no rush as I caressed his head and along his back, slowly stroking him. The room was quiet as he gradually sank into his role. By the time I slid on his mitts, I could see that more of the stress had faded.

Excitement built as I picked up the lube. Anticipation of the pleasure, yes, but I knew he was also excited to cross those last few steps and let his puppy persona take over. The sound of the lube sent a shiver through Sawyer, but his head relaxed down. He was so different from Cooper but so similar in many ways. Every day it felt like I got to know them better.

Bringing my slick fingers to his opening, I circled around the tight ring of muscles for several long seconds until I eased one finger in. Taking my time, I slowly pressed deeper, letting his body adjust and making sure he knew it was about relaxation and nothing else.

I could see his length thicken, but I ignored it, focusing instead on running one hand down his back and over his ass and down his leg. Gradually, the muscles in his body loosened even more, and after a while, I slid in a second finger.

The base of the tail wasn't that thick, so it didn't take long to finish getting him ready. When I pulled my fingers out, he gave a whine. It was clearly a sound of protest, but one that I associated more with his puppy persona than his human side.

Trying not to smile, I brought the plug up to his body and started easing it in. He gave the tail a wag and stretched his back up as his body adjusted to the sensation. Grabbing a tissue off the nightstand, I wiped my hands and reached for his collar. By the time I brought it up to his neck, he had the sleepy, satisfied look that I'd come to associate with his pup.

Where Cooper's puppy side was enthusiastic and excitable and always aroused, Sawyer's was calm and cuddly. When the collar was buckled around his neck and he was already deep into his puppy persona, I stood and leaned down to attach his leash. We didn't always play with it, but something about it felt right to me. I wanted him to know that he wasn't alone. "Come, Chance."

If Chance had been a biological dog, he would have been perfect as an emotional support animal. He had a calm demeanor that would have been wonderful for that type of field. Unfortunately, there wasn't anything like that in the puppy play community.

Part of me thought there should be, but I realized the average person wouldn't see that as the most traditional way to play in the lifestyle. As we walked out to the living room, we both fell into our roles. I wasn't Sawyer's lover any longer; I was Chance's master, and I was going to curl up with my pup for the afternoon.

"Up, Chance." When he was settled on the couch, I sat down and stretched my legs out, my feet up on the coffee table. "Come here, Chance."

Chance settled against me, using my thigh as a pillow, and closed his eyes. As I reached for the remote and flicked through the channels, I absently caressed over his head and down his back and side.

It was a perfect way to spend an afternoon.

If someone had described the scene to me several months ago, I would have thought they were crazy. But as I sat there, curled up with my sweet pup, I felt a wash of emotion come over me. Sawyer trusted me enough to show me a side that most people would never see. It was more open and intimate than anything we could ever do in the bedroom. Watching my sweet pup relax and share himself with me made me love him even more.

"I KNOW COOPER WOULD'VE HATED IT, BUT THAT WAS delicious." Sawyer leaned back in the seat with a big grin on his face. "It's worth bringing up sushi just to hear him whine and go on about how gross it is."

Smiling, I shook my head. "You're as bad as he is when it comes to teasing and driving each other crazy."

"But the difference is that he deserves it." Sawyer's big grin said he was teasing, but there was at least a little bit of truth in his sentence. Of course, most of the time Cooper *wanted* to be punished, so that had to be taken into consideration as well.

Sawyer only did it when he was at his most relaxed and stress-free.

Evidently, he was feeling wonderful after a quiet day and a delicious dinner, because he'd spent the last hour smiling and flirting and teasing. It was a side I didn't get to see very often. "What do you think? Should we tell him that we forgot his dessert at the table?" Sawyer's eyes danced in delight.

I turned back to focus on the road, shaking my head again. "Do you really want him pouting all night? You went to all that work making him a delicious dessert."

Sawyer couldn't seem to decide if he wanted to mess with Cooper or not. "Maybe not."

He sat up in the seat, and I glanced over to see a huge grin on his face. "Maybe we should be finishing up a piece as he comes in and tell him that we decided to save him a couple of bites."

Laughing, I reached over and put my hand on his leg, giving it a squeeze. "You're devious tonight."

"Just a little bit." Sawyer settled back in his seat giving me a very Cooper-ish smile.

I let my fingers wander up his leg toward his groin, teasing, but not actually touching his cock. "I can think of much better ways to drive Cooper crazy."

Sawyer shivered, and a little moan escaped. "What kind of ways?"

I inched my hand further up his leg, barely caressing his dick, but it seemed to be getting harder without much physical contact. "Well, I seem to remember promising you a spanking. I think Cooper would love to watch your ass get reddened, but I can think of quite a few ways to include him that would have him turned on and frustrated. I think that would be much better than making him pout over cheesecake."

Sawyer made a breathy little sound, and he nodded. "Cooper likes watching."

"Yes, it's going to make him beautifully hard." And I knew exactly how to make the best use of his erection.

I was going to drive both my boys crazy.

I inched my hand up again until I could feel his erection. Caressing his leg, I focused on the road, listening to the hitch in his breathing and the feel of his body as he tensed, trying to stay still. "Do you want a spanking while Cooper watches? Do you want to be naked across my lap while he sees you hard and squirming?"

The way his erection jerked under my fingers, I already knew the answer. It took him a moment to find the words, however. Sawyer's voice was low and needy, but there was still that hint of hesitation. "Yes, please."

"You want to let everything go, don't you? I'm going to make you feel so good and send you flying." Another moan escaped Sawyer into the darkness of the car. I didn't want to push him too far, but it was easy to picture opening up his pants at the next stoplight and stroking him as we drove home.

I saw Sawyer nod out of the corner of my eye, and I caressed around the sensitive head of his erection as a reward. More needy sounds poured out of him before he could find the words to respond. "Yes, Master. It feels so good when you do that."

"Cooper and I both love seeing you come completely undone. Having you spread out over my lap while we get to play with you is going to be perfect. Maybe if you're very good, I'll spank you long enough that you'll feel it tomorrow. Would you like that?" The shiver that raced through him said he liked the idea as much as I did.

"Running errands and walking through the store still being

able to feel my hand on your body would be incredible, wouldn't it?" Sawyer wasn't the natural exhibitionist Cooper was, but something about the fantasy appealed to him.

His hips thrust out, pressing his erection harder against my hand, making me chuckle. "But just so I'm fair, if you go to the store with a red ass, then I'm going to need to do something special with Cooper. Won't I? Maybe I'll put the cock cage back on him, or maybe I'll slide a nice long plug inside of him before we go. What do you think?"

Sawyer gave a deep moan. Yes, he liked that idea.

As I slowly caressed the head of his erection, Sawyer's hands moved to grip the seat. I hadn't kept him hard *all* day, but between his time as a pup and all the teasing touches and kisses I'd given him, there'd been a constant stream of love, and arousal, from him. Sparking that heat into a flame was easier than both of us expected.

It took him a long moment before he answered. I could hear the need in his voice. It would have been unmistakable, even if I hadn't been able to feel the evidence of his desire. "Yes, he'd want to be teased too. He'd like both. Cooper would love for you to keep him soft but make it so his body wanted to get hard."

A slightly strangled chuckle escaped Sawyer as he continued. "Maybe it will keep him so distracted that we'll end up getting out of there without too much weird stuff in the cart."

He had a point. Cooper was not the easiest person to grocery shop with. But if I kept his mind on his caged dick, then it would probably be a more entertaining trip for all of us. "Yes, I think you'd like that too. And I think you'd like knowing he was trapped and turned on. I think it would make you even more aroused as well."

As I finished speaking, we pulled up to a stoplight, and I turned to Sawyer. Giving his dick a squeeze, I leaned over and kissed him tenderly on the cheek. He moaned and gave me a heated look as the mixed signals seemed to send him higher. Something on my face made him sigh in frustration.

"I'm going to have so much fun playing with my sexy boys tonight." The images running through my head were beautiful and wicked. Just like my boys.

Sawyer groaned and shook his head. "You're going to make us crazy."

Nodding, I smiled devilishly. "And you're going to love every minute of it."

7

COOPER

"THEY'D BETTER BE NAKED and covered in cake." After all the fantasies I'd had at work, anything less would be a disappointment. "Whipped cream might work too."

I wasn't going to be picky as long as someone was naked.

The drive home seemed to take forever. The fact that I'd only gotten vague text messages about what they'd been up to had made my imagination go into overdrive. I'd stopped bugging them, though, when Sawyer had started texting the pictures of their sushi.

Gross.

"That might end up being too sticky to eat off anyone. Oh, a chocolate pie might work." So maybe I was hungry.

And overcaffeinated.

Not that I would tell them that. For a Saturday afternoon, the coffee shop had been packed. One person after another had made it difficult to get a full break. It wouldn't have been that bad, but we were slightly short-staffed again.

We'd finally gotten everyone healthy, but there were a thousand things people had needed time off for lately. I'd had to make do with grabbing bites of my lunch when I could, and I'd made up for the lack of food with too much coffee.

"We could just have sex in the kitchen and dessert afterward. That might work too." Sex and ice cream would be as good as sex and pancakes.

As I pulled into the driveway and parked the car, I was racing toward the house in seconds. I pictured Sawyer laid out on the floor, hard and naked. But it would be just as hot with Jackson on the couch and Sawyer riding him.

I smiled when I actually had to dig my key out to open the door. "I'm so proud of you."

The house was quiet as I shut the door behind me, re-locking it. They'd actually remembered to secure the door. It was a skill we were still working on with Jackson.

Laughter came from the kitchen, and I heard Jackson's voice calling out. "You haven't seen what we did yet. Why are you so proud of us?"

Grinning, I threw my stuff on the side table and headed toward the kitchen. Sawyer could be laid out on the table. That would probably keep things neater. "You remembered to lock the door!"

They were both sitting at the table, fully clothed. It was slightly disappointing until I saw what was in front of them. "Cheesecake! Did you guys go to the store today? Was it that bakery downtown? It looks delicious. Where's my piece?"

Sawyer seemed to sit up straighter in his chair as he smiled, but Jackson laughed and beamed. Holding out his arms, he pushed back from the table. "Come here. How much coffee have you had?"

Shit.

"You didn't answer my question." And that had to work because I certainly wasn't answering *his* unless I had to.

Jackson laughed knowingly as I climbed on his lap and straddled his legs. "We made it."

Smiling, I gave him a kiss and glanced over at Sawyer. "But what brand is it? It looks better than the last one."

They both chuckled and for some reason, Sawyer blushed. What was dirty about cheesecake? We were just talking about eating it, right? Before I could ask, Jackson spoke. "No, we went to the store and bought the ingredients, then made it from scratch."

"Like with cheese and...stuff?" What actually went into cheesecake?

They called it a cake, but it looked like a wiggly pie.

Jackson laughed so hard he nearly toppled us both out of the chair. When he could finally breathe, he kissed my forehead, smiling. "Are you picturing it made out of cheddar cheese or something?"

I snorted and shook my head. "No. White cheese, *duh*."

That set him off again. I was mostly kidding, but I had no idea what the dessert was made of. "Where's my piece, funny guy?"

Sawyer was grinning and shaking his head at the two of us. But Sawyer didn't tease. He probably hadn't known what went in it either before they'd started baking it. "I'll get it."

By the time Sawyer had gotten the cake out of the fridge, I'd grabbed a glass of water and Jackson had managed to control himself. "I'll show you how to make it next time, but it's things like cream cheese and eggs."

"It looks like a cream soup before you bake it, but it turns out right in the end." Sawyer shrugged and took a bite of his dessert.

Jackson kissed me as I stood and rearranged myself on his lap again. "I'm not going anywhere. You're comfortable."

As I sat down, I gave him a long look. "Did you brush your teeth? I saw that fishy stuff you were eating."

That started him off again, but it didn't answer my question. "We had the discussion about sushi and kissing."

Leaning back in the chair, he finally stopped laughing and grinned. "Yes, we both brushed our teeth just for you."

I gave him a quick peck before I turned and cut off a big piece of my cheesecake. "Because you're humoring the crazy guy or because you're hoping to get lucky?"

Sawyer answered immediately. "Both."

I waggled my eyebrows at him as I swallowed. "Are you still getting a spanking?"

He looked a little shy when he nodded, but he wasn't as nervous as he'd been in the past. "Yes."

I smiled as I cut off another piece. "And you waited for me? Aww." I leaned over and puckered my lips.

Sawyer laughed and stretched out to give me the kiss I was not so subtly hinting for. Settling back into Jackson's arms, I glanced at the two of them. "How was your day?"

As we ate, they talked about baking the cake and grocery shopping and all the little things about their day. "Did you do a big trip? We're out of almost everything."

Sawyer shook his head, but Jackson answered. "No, we talked about it and decided to all go together tomorrow."

I nodded and gave Jackson a kiss on the cheek. "Probably a good idea. You forgot the whole frozen food section last time."

Sawyer snorted. "You're no better. You skipped out on all the vegetables and came home with nothing but cereal and microwave burritos."

I resembled that remark, but I wasn't going to admit it.

They'd made the mistake of sending me hungry. "I wasn't that bad, and it wasn't my fault. I had green beans and pasta in there too. You shouldn't send me to the store without a list."

Jackson was grinning like we were both lunatics. Before Sawyer could think up a comeback, Jackson broke in. "Are we really going to debate who's the worst grocery shopper after every one of us came home with milk last week?"

The water I was drinking almost came out of my nose when I snorted. "That was so funny."

Sawyer laughed. "We still have two gallons left."

"See, we need more cereal." What else could you do with that much milk? Nobody in the house even liked it in their coffee. Everyone preferred creamier options.

It was Jackson's turn to chuckle. "We still have several boxes. Maybe we can make French toast or rice pudding with the extra milk before it goes bad."

I couldn't remember ever eating rice pudding, but I wasn't an idiot. I knew what it was.

Mostly.

Still, it was too good an opportunity to pass up. "Why would anyone make pudding and put rice in it? Wouldn't it be like lumpy snot?"

Sawyer's water came out his nose.

Oops.

Jackson laughed so hard I really did fall off his lap. Those lightning reflexes of his were the only thing that kept me from landing on my ass. But it would've been worth it to see the look on Sawyer's face. He'd been too stressed and serious lately.

By the time we'd cleaned up the mess, and I finished my dessert—both servings—we were all thinking about the naughty promises Jackson had made. He'd kept what he wanted to do a secret, though. He'd given vague hints about a spanking for Sawyer but smiled when he'd looked at me. I couldn't decide what that meant, but it sent a shiver down my spine.

When he gave us both long kisses and told us to go get a shower and meet him back in the bedroom, I knew it was going to be good.

When his touch lingered and the wicked glint in his eye only got brighter, it made my toes curl.

When he told us to wash *thoroughly*, I might have moaned.

I had the fastest shower in history—though I followed his directions and washed *everything* I could think of *incredibly* thoroughly.

"Done!" Running back in from the guest room, I did a big *ta-da* entrance.

Jackson was leaning back against the headboard, still dressed, but looking sexy and dominant. Something about the way he watched me with the slightest smirk had my already hard cock even more excited. Little Cooper—well, not really little—he'd liked the *thorough* cleaning.

And I loved *fabulous* instructions.

"You look a little bit excited, pup." Jackson's teasing words sent my anticipation higher.

Telling him I was excited for my punishment seemed… wrong…and a bit dangerous by the look on his face. "I wanted to make you proud and not dawdle."

True—and it was a much safer answer than telling him I was horny and ready to come.

"I'm glad you want to be good for me." The look in his eyes said that I was going to have that desire tested fairly shortly.

When we'd first started dating Jackson, he'd said that he'd always assumed he was pretty vanilla. It hadn't taken long for him to realize that he was more interesting than he'd thought. He'd taken to role-play and domination in general like a duck to water. It was incredible.

"Thank you, Master."

Before I could say anything or finish climbing onto the bed, Sawyer came out of the bathroom. He was naked too but not in a flashy way…he was just naked. And hard. But not in an *I have a fabulous dick* kind of way.

I was the only one with style in the house some days.

"I'm ready, Master." Sawyer's words were quiet and even, but I could hear the excitement just under the surface. He was trying so hard to be calm. That was the biggest giveaway of how much he wanted it.

"My boys look perfect. Come here, Sawyer. We're going to get you both ready, and then it will be time for your spanking." Jackson said it too straightforwardly. I couldn't wait to see what he was up to.

"Yes, Master." Sawyer walked over to the bed, and I finished climbing up.

Jackson gave the mattress a pat on one side and nodded at me. Taking it to mean that he wanted me beside him, I kept crawling over. Sawyer got the same gesture, just on the other side of the bed.

What was he up to?

"All right, we're going to get Cooper ready first. You needed to be punished, didn't you? I think we need to help you remember how to follow directions."

Fuck. It was going to be incredible.

"Yes, Master." It was all I could do to stay still and look reasonably well-behaved. I wanted to bounce all over the bed like a five-year-old after too much sugar.

Jackson's eyes sparkled, and I knew he understood how excited I was. He'd gotten so good at teasing us. I loved it.

When he turned back to Sawyer, his expression was as heated but more tender. "And you're going to get a spanking. Not because you've been naughty, but just because I want to see that sexy ass of yours nice and pink, and I want you to remember how important you are to me."

Aww, he was so cute.

Sawyer's dick jerked, but he nodded slowly. "Yes, Master."

Jackson reached out with both hands and caressed our cocks, giving them a few slow strokes as a reward. "My good boys."

I might have whimpered—just a little.

Jackson gave a low chuckle as he removed his hands from

our erections. "We're going to get Cooper ready first, so come a little closer."

I wasn't sure what he would do, but I inched closer until he nodded. Pressed up against his leg, I waited as he reached behind Sawyer and grabbed something off the nightstand. I should have done less *ta-da*-ing and paid more attention when I'd walked in.

With his free hand, Jackson wrapped his fingers around the base of my dick and angled it upward. "Sawyer, bend over and see if your mouth can get him any harder. I want him so erect he's aching."

Sawyer immediately mumbled a low, "Yes, Master," before bending over onto all fours. Stretched out beside Master, Sawyer's ass was offered up beautifully. When Sawyer's lips wrapped around me, Jackson's hand reached out and made long, slow strokes over Sawyer's cheeks.

Between the incredible feeling of Sawyer's mouth and the visual of Jackson touching him so possessively, it wasn't long until I was so hard I just wanted to thrust my cock into his mouth and come. Unfortunately, that was when Sawyer released my dick and sat up.

His focus immediately went to Jackson, which was incredibly hot. "He's ready, Master."

Jackson nodded and gave Sawyer a look like he was pleased his boy had followed directions. When Jackson moved his hand back to my cock to evaluate Sawyer's work, I groaned. The pleasure was too good. Jackson gave me a wicked smile and nodded. "Yes, I think that will do."

The hand that had been caressing Sawyer moved to the bed, and for the first time, I realized what he'd grabbed from the nightstand. A cock ring. "Goodie!" probably wouldn't have been the right response, so I kept my mouth shut.

We both watched as Jackson wrapped the strip of leather around my dick and secured it tightly. It wasn't painful, but I wouldn't go soft anytime soon. The number of possibilities that flashed through my head were staggering, and I couldn't decide what I wanted most.

Jackson gave my dick a pat and watched as my erection bobbed. Sensations flooded through me, and I moaned again, making him chuckle. "Very good. All right, Cooper, turn around and bend over. You're not done yet."

"Yes, Master." Not wanting to miss a single thing he would do to me, I turned around quickly and bent over on all fours.

"Head down on the mattress and offer your ass up to me." Jackson gave my butt a light smack when I didn't follow directions quick enough. It sent sparks through me, and I wanted to beg for more, but I knew I wouldn't be the one spanked that day.

It was Sawyer's turn.

When I was in position, Jackson made approving noises, and I felt a shift on the bed. Sawyer's hands reached out and caressed along my back and down over my ass to my legs. I wasn't sure if it was supposed to help me relax or turn me on more, but it was some kind of combination of the two.

Sawyer's hands kept caressing me as Jackson brought one finger to my hole. He teased around the ring of muscle for a moment before he pressed it into me. Relaxing as best I could, his finger slid in easily and started the slow, methodical process of stretching me. Jackson didn't seem to be in any hurry, which only made everything more intense.

After a few long moments, Jackson removed his finger. I'd expected to feel another finger slide in but after a few seconds, I felt something more rigid pressing against me. It was slender and long as it entered me, and it wasn't until it was pressing against my prostate that I realized what he'd grabbed—that damned prostate massaging plug.

God, I loved Jackson.

It was an evil little toy that we'd recently purchased. It

wasn't meant to stretch someone's hole; it was meant to drive people crazy. When it was fully seated, and my ass was clenched around the base, securing it tightly, Jackson gave me another pat. "That's perfect."

Whatever he'd planned would end up being the most devious punishment ever. I just knew it.

"Turn around again, Cooper. I need you to move a little bit lower because I want Sawyer stretched out across the bed." Jackson had Sawyer move to the other side where I'd been kneeling. With a few quick instructions, he had Sawyer's dick between his thighs and Sawyer's ass offered up beautifully.

"Sawyer, spread your legs. Cooper, kneel between." We'd been in similar positions in the past, and I was beginning to get an idea of what he wanted, but I knew I was missing something. It wasn't quite obvious enough yet.

When we were both in position, instead of starting the spanking, Jackson reached over to the nightstand again. When he grabbed the lube, it was unexpected—unexpected but interesting. I watched as he slicked up his fingers and brought his hand to Sawyer's ass.

Sawyer gave a moan as Jackson teased around his hole. As Jackson slid one finger into him, a shiver ran through Sawyer and his ass arched up more. He seemed as curious as I was, but we both knew better than to ask. Jackson was creative, but he never pushed the limits of what we were comfortable with.

As Sawyer adjusted, Jackson added the second. The room was quiet with the only noises being the dirty, almost wet sound of the lube and Sawyer's moans of pleasure. When Jackson added a third, I knew Sawyer was getting something thicker than a plug.

I was starting to get a good idea about what kind of toy Jackson would be using on Sawyer.

Me.

The idea was so perfect, my cock jerked and a shiver raced

through me. Jackson looked up at me and gave me a knowing smile. I got a little nod before he went back to focusing on Sawyer. It was almost painful to watch.

The waiting.

Knowing how good it would feel to Sawyer.

Knowing how good it would feel to me.

How frustrating it would be when I didn't get to come.

I was going to be the real-life dildo that Jackson used to fuck Sawyer with during his spanking.

Fuck.

The ideas and dirty images that flashed through my mind would have been enough to make me come without the cock ring. When he thought Sawyer was ready, or maybe when he knew he couldn't push Sawyer any further, Jackson removed his fingers and took an unreasonably long time cleaning off his hand.

We were both shaking in anticipation as Jackson rubbed slow circles over Sawyer's cheeks. "You're going to get a nice long spanking. Just what you wanted. But to make this more fun and because Cooper was naughty, I'm going to break up your spanking by having him slide deep inside you. How does that sound?"

We both moaned. Sawyer found his words first, though. "Yes, Master. Yes, that sounds…please."

Okay, he found some of his words. Not that I was doing much better.

I'd been focused on Sawyer for so long that I'd forgotten about the toy. The way the bed moved when Jackson's hand came down to spank Sawyer had the memory rushing forward again. With each smack, the mattress would shift as they both moved, jostling me just enough to push the toy into my prostate. Lightning would go off through me each time, and the beautiful scene in front of me only made it worse.

It felt like an eternity, but it wasn't long before Jackson stopped and rubbed the slow circles on Sawyer's ass again. "Come here, Cooper. Yes, slowly, I don't want him to come yet. If you do a good job and follow directions, I might let you later but then again, I might not. You're going to have to show me how good you can be."

The tempting promise bounced around in my head as I inched forward. Hearing him explicitly say that I might not get to come made everything more erotic. Master was the only one who could decide when my punishment was over.

Each movement had the toy shifting inside me. As I stretched out over Sawyer, I groaned. It was going to drive me insane. But that was kind of the point. I wasn't sure if as Jackson's toy I would get to kiss Sawyer, so I stayed just above him and focused on his hole. His body arched beautifully as I inched in. He made needy noises and his hips seemed to offer his hole up, begging for more.

Wanting to follow directions, I kept the pace slow, sinking in as far as the cock ring would allow. But when Jackson reached over to the nightstand and grabbed the remote for the plug, I knew he wasn't planning on taking it easy on me.

The first vibrations sent shockwaves through me, and I gasped. I hadn't realized I was fucking Sawyer too fast until Jackson brought one hand up and tweaked my nipple. "Naughty boy, slow down. This isn't for you."

We both moaned in frustration as I slowed down. "Yes, Master. I'm sorry." It took every bit of focus I had to respond. All I wanted to do was race toward the pleasure.

Unfortunately, Jackson had a different idea. "All right, that's enough. I'm not done with his spanking."

Slowly pulling out of Sawyer, I straightened and kneeled between his legs as Jackson started spanking him again. That time the movement of the mattress wasn't noticeable at all because the vibrations coming from the toy were too strong. All

I could do was watch and try to be good enough that he would let me come.

Eventually.

After a few more minutes, Jackson used my cock again to pleasure Sawyer. Round after round, we went through the perfect torture. Sometimes he would turn the toy off. Sometimes he would turn the toy up, but there was always the feeling of being filled and left hard, knowing it would never be enough.

When Sawyer's ass was reddened, and Jackson seemed satisfied with how it looked and how lost in sensations Sawyer was, he gave me a nod. "All right, Cooper. Let's see if you can make him come."

Make him come.

Jackson said nothing about my need, so as I began making love to Sawyer, I tried not to think about it. It was impossible, though. Everything was all tangled up in my head, and it was incredible. Wave after wave of desire went through me as the vibrations intensified, but all I wanted to focus on was Sawyer. If I made him come and showed master I could behave, he might let me orgasm.

The promise kept the pleasure just out of reach but temptingly close.

Sawyer had started out moaning, but as the spanking had gone on, the sounds had turned needier and more desperate. As I fucked him, I could feel his body shaking and clenching around me, but he was too lost to make anything more than the low sexy noises that escaped.

Jackson shifted and I knew that he'd tightened his thighs around Sawyer's erection. That little shift was enough to send Sawyer flying. His body arched and his muscles contracted around me as I pushed into him faster and harder, nailing his prostate with each thrust.

Shivers raced through me as I watched Sawyer. The

restraint around my dick was the only thing that kept me from following him. I probably should've been grateful that it kept me from getting in trouble, but I was too lost inside my head.

All I wanted to do was come.

All I wanted to do was to hear Jackson give me permission.

I needed to hear the words from Master. As Sawyer's orgasm faded, he slumped down onto Jackson's lap, and I slowly eased out of him. My hips thrust, trying to fuck the air as I turned my focus to Jackson. I wanted to be good, but I started to beg.

"Please, Master. Please, can I..." The words were lost as Jackson's hands reached out and stroked my still-slick cock.

"You were very good. Can you see how incredible Sawyer feels? Do you want to come now?" I could see in his heated gaze that the question was there to drive me crazy, but I nodded frantically.

"Yes, please." I clamped my lips down trying not to beg any further.

When he released the cock ring, my body almost didn't know what to do. I was shaking and hard as he slowly stroked my cock. It wasn't until he turned on the vibrations again and squeezed down on my erection that the dam burst.

Just as he started to give the order to come, my orgasm exploded through me. Wave after wave of pleasure seemed to short-circuit everything in my body. All I could do was shake and frantically thrust into his clenched fist.

When the pleasure was finally over, I slumped down on the bed next to Jackson. Sawyer was trapped, but he didn't seem to mind. He chuckled, but he made no move to get up. We were both thoroughly exhausted.

Jackson leaned over and kissed my forehead, smiling tenderly. "You are both so beautiful. I love you."

Sawyer's words of love were sweet and tender as he sent them back to Jackson. My mind hadn't caught up with everything yet, so all I could do was give him a dopey smile and nod my head. "Love you. Devious master. Love. Wicked."

I closed my eyes and listened as Jackson chuckled. His warm, rough hands caressed us in long slow strokes that made me feel wanted and loved. He was always like that. Every word and every touch seemed to radiate how much he loved us and how much he wanted us right there beside him.

8

SAWYER

"WHY DO we need three boxes of cereal? We're shopping for a week or two, not the apocalypse." Shopping with Cooper was like picking out groceries with a sugared up, overcaffeinated monkey.

But it was hard to stay frustrated when he got so excited.

He turned and gave me a too sweet, too eager expression. There was at least a fifty percent chance it was fake. "But I like cereal for breakfast. And when I'm home during the day, it makes a quick lunch."

Yep, completely fake. And so was that argument.

"When you're home during the day, Jackson makes you lunch." Even if Jackson couldn't make him something to eat, there were usually plenty of leftovers. Jackson liked to make sure there was enough for us to take to work when we needed to.

Jackson was chuckling, not ready to take a side yet. I glanced down at the boxes in the cart and the one in Cooper's hands. "Put the chocolate one back—that's got to be dessert anyway."

He didn't need any more sugar in his life. Between all the

crap he snuck at work and all the little things he convinced Jackson to make for him, he was constantly on a sugar high. "Two boxes. That's it. If you honestly feel the need for a third, then it should be healthy."

Jackson gave Cooper a small nod and Cooper huffed. "Cereal should be fun, not something with the words fiber, bran, or regularity on the cover."

He didn't argue with Jackson, however.

The chocolate cereal went back on the shelf, and he started browsing again. I'd have had more patience if we hadn't been in that aisle for at least five minutes already. He was looking for a box of cereal, not the most perfect, unblemished apple he could find.

As Cooper moved toward the healthier options, Jackson smiled. "I'm not sure I've ever seen a box of cereal with the word regularity on the front."

Cooper was trying not to giggle, but he was losing the battle. Finally, he grabbed up a box of granola that had to have been healthier than the sugary kid cereals and put it in the cart. "Perfect."

I wouldn't have called it perfect, but it would work.

As we finished walking down the aisle, Jackson stopped the cart to grab some oatmeal. Cooper and I didn't mind it, although we'd eaten a lot of oatmeal in the past because it was so cheap. But Cooper's eyes lit up when he realized that he might be able to get one of the fun kinds. Adding sugar and sparkly things to oatmeal might have made it taste better, but it also quadrupled the price, so we'd always stuck with something simple.

Jackson chuckled, listening to Cooper's impassioned arguments about the benefits of oatmeal with some kind of little marshmallows or sugary eggs in them. After all the crap that he put in the cart, there was no way Jackson was going to give in to him. Cooper seemed to be realizing that, but he also saw that

Jackson thought it was funny, so he wasn't going to give up on his bit just yet.

Until he ran into the other cart, that is.

"But you said it had to be healthy, and I've been such a good —oh," Cooper turned to look at the cart that had rounded the corner quickly. "I'm sor—"

The words seemed to stick in his throat, and he stood there staring, the box of oatmeal still in his hand. I wasn't in much better shape. Jackson looked concerned, glancing between the two of us. It was clear he had no idea what was going on.

As many stories as we'd told him about our families, he'd never seen any pictures.

Cooper had a few tucked away in a box, but it wasn't something he brought out very often. If I'd ever thought we would have seen anyone from our past again, I might have insisted on it just to prepare Jackson. But I never imagined I'd be standing in the grocery store in front of Cooper's parents.

I'd actually thought we had a better chance of running into aliens on a deserted road then seeing his family again.

They didn't seem to be doing much better. His mother was quiet but had a shocked look on her face. His dad, on the other hand, looked slightly constipated. Maybe he needed some of Cooper's regularity cereal.

Jackson knew something was wrong, but until someone else made the first move, I had a feeling he would just be patient. A toddler screamed on the other side of the store, breaking the standoff. Cooper's mother opened her mouth, but his dad spoke first. "I see that you haven't decided to change your lifestyle."

His mother frowned, but his dad pushed the cart, moving them both forward. "Come on, we did everything we could to impress upon him that there are some things we won't stomach."

His dad was still clearly an asshole, but something about his mother's expression had me questioning what she was thinking.

She didn't say anything to Cooper, and she didn't comment on what her husband was saying, so I still thought she was a crazy bitch, but...

Cooper finally moved, but it was just to put the oatmeal back.

I was lost. "Cooper, I'm..."

Cooper interrupted, shaking his head. "It's fine."

But it wasn't fine.

I'd have thought we were far enough away from where his family used to live that we wouldn't have run into them. Who grocery shops forty-five minutes away from home? I tried to think back to the items in their cart, and I couldn't picture anything specifically. There'd just been a couple of items. Were they visiting someone? Had there been some kind of party or social event on this side of town they'd wanted to attend?

Jackson grabbed the oatmeal off the shelf and put it in the cart. "Come here, baby."

It was clear he was starting to understand what had happened, and I knew there had to be a thousand questions running through his mind. He didn't ask any, though. Jackson just gathered Cooper in his arms and gave him a tight hug. Cooper let his head rest against Jackson's shoulder for just a moment before straightening. "So I can have anything I want in the store?"

It was like watching the movie and knowing that the DVD had skipped, and you'd missed a few lines. He didn't glance back at his parents or even mention them. Cooper smiled at Jackson and then peered into the cart.

"Of course, baby." Jackson ran his hand over Cooper's head before letting Cooper step away. "Whatever you want."

Not knowing what to do or what to say was perfectly reasonable, especially since he hadn't been there when all the crazy had initially unfolded. But giving Cooper free rein in the grocery store was insane.

No amount of trauma was worth that. "Within reason. Whatever he wants within reason."

Cooper giggled, still ignoring the scene that had just transpired. "If we ever do have an apocalypse, the first thing we're doing is coming to the grocery store, so I can get all the fun stuff."

"Deal. But when the zombies are attacking and all we have to survive on is marshmallows and chocolate cereal, we're going to eat you first." Okay, so maybe not the best way to handle things, but in my defense, making him laugh seemed like a better idea than trying to figure out what to say.

Cooper turned and gave us both a teasing grin. "I'd be delicious."

Jackson seemed stumped and I couldn't blame him. Finally, he seemed to come to some kind of mental decision. "This conversation has taken a turn toward the absurd and slightly creepy. If you want me to pick out any meat to grill or even any bacon to cook for breakfast you're going to stop talking about eating Cooper." He shivered and looked a little like Cooper talking about sushi.

I gave Cooper a teasing frown. "I just can't take you anywhere."

"Hey, you were the one who was talking about cannibalization." Cooper must have decided that if we were going to get in trouble, he would throw me under the bus.

Jackson shivered again and actually looked kind of green. "Okay, no more of that."

Even Cooper looked at him like he'd done something interesting. "So I shouldn't mention that my ass is big enough it could probably be a really good roast?"

Jackson actually gagged. He was so funny. He was worse than Cooper with the sushi.

Not wanting to have to clean up vomit in the grocery store, I poked Cooper. "If you keep doing that, he's going to make you put the cereal back, and you're just going to end up with plain oatmeal and some of those boxes of fiber cereal."

Cooper pouted and looked toward the cart possessively. "Okay, I'll behave."

He ruined the innocent act when he looked up at Jackson sweetly. "So I shouldn't ask for ham for dinner this week?"

"Cooper!" We were all distracted again, which was probably his goal, but Jackson really did look an unhealthy shade of green.

"No more, I promise. I'll be good." I had a feeling Cooper wouldn't be able to keep that promise.

Stress made me uncomfortable, and the awkward situation made Jackson confused, but Cooper seemed determined to handle everything with humor. And sugar. If we got out of the grocery store without an entire cabinet full of crap and Jackson barfing everywhere, it would be a miracle.

"Two cartons of ice cream, a box of cookies, and three packages of gum are not going to make up for the fact that his parents are assholes." I whispered the words low as we unloaded the car. Cooper had already taken in several bags, and it was the first chance I'd had to speak with Jackson alone.

"I know, but it made him smile." Jackson looked sad and glanced back toward the house.

He was such a sweet enabler. "That's not the point."

Okay, so maybe it was the point, but we'd come out of the store with more junk food than real food. Somebody would have to make another run to the grocery store later in the week to make sure we had enough food for dinner. "How about we make him talk the problem out instead of just doing things to make him smile?"

Jackson's expression was still troubled, but the corners of

his mouth turned up slightly, and he kissed my forehead. "You're right."

It was clear neither of us was looking forward to the conversation.

"Come on, before all this ice cream melts." I shook my head at the number of bags in the back of the car.

As he grabbed several of them, Jackson snorted. "Stop pretending you were more of a grown-up in the store than me. You didn't tell him no either."

I was pretty sure I had tried to rein him in several times before the disastrous meeting in the cereal aisle. After that, it was debatable. "I said he couldn't have that third carton of ice cream."

Jackson shook his head, and his expression softened to a real smile, some of the sadness fading from his eyes. "Um, no, you said a third carton wouldn't fit. That's not the same thing."

Yes, it was. "At least I said no to something. You were the one who let him have too much gum."

Jackson barked out a laugh, starting for the porch. "They were small packs."

Cooper had him wrapped around his little finger. It was so cute. "Have you ever even seen him chew gum?"

Jackson had to think about it as he climbed the stairs. "Um, no. But that's not the point. He had fun picking them out."

I gave Jackson a wink as I followed him into the house. If he wanted to pretend he hadn't been played, then I wouldn't burst his bubble. "If he falls asleep with it in his mouth and gets it in his hair, you have to deal with it."

Jackson was still smiling as we walked into the kitchen. "I think we're more likely to find wrappers everywhere."

"What?" Cooper's head popped out of the fridge. "I think we're going to have to rearrange some things if we have much more that needs to go in here. It's getting kind of full."

Entirely too much yogurt, cheese, and luncheon meat would do that to any fridge.

Shaking his head, Jackson set the bags down on the table. "I think the rest of the stuff goes in the freezer or the pantry."

"Good. There's still a bit of room in the freezer."

"If some of the meat doesn't fit, then we'll barbecue it later or cook it tomorrow." Jackson had recovered by the time we'd gotten around to the meat department, but he'd refused to consider the roasts and had skipped over the bacon entirely.

We'd ended up with a variety of steaks and chicken that Jackson had given several long looks to before he'd agreed to the purchase. Evidently boneless, skinless chicken looked gross after a conversation on cannibalism, but anything on the bone was fine. Figuring out dinners would be interesting for a while.

"Your mother said she wanted everyone to get together again, didn't she?" Cooper started rummaging through the grocery bags, looking for things to go in the freezer.

Jackson began carrying items to the pantry and nodded. "Yes, that's what she said when she called the other day. But she's not at the point of threatening yet."

Cooper laughed. "Why don't we see if they want us to bring some of the chicken over later?" He looked at the package in his hand turning it over several times. "You can put this on the grill, right?"

Jackson turned to him and smiled. "Yes, you can." Then he looked over at me. "Sawyer, what do you think? Does that sound good?"

I was still firmly convinced that someone should've said no to Cooper in the grocery store, but if they wanted to have dinner with Jackson's family, that was fine with me. "Sure."

Cooper had a bounce in his step as he went back to the table and rummaged around in the bags. "Did we get some potato salad? That would go good with the chicken."

We'd grabbed all kinds of crazy, so no matter what he pulled out of the bags, it wouldn't surprise me. "There are still a few more in the car. I'll go get those while you look. But don't forget to keep putting things away."

Cooper gave me an innocent smile. "What? We're doing a good job."

Jackson snickered. "He's not going to fall for that again."

"No distracting him with blowjobs or anything else. I'll be right back." Those two could not be trusted alone for a second.

"You're going out to the car. You're not running errands for the rest of the afternoon." Cooper tried to keep the sweet, honest expression going, but his giggle ruined it.

"I know you. It might not take you a full minute to have both of you naked. I do not want to come back in here and see you two having sex over the groceries." And as crazy as that statement sounded, even to me, it was not the first time I'd had to say it.

Cooper laughed, not making any promises, but Jackson nodded. "We'll do our best. Just don't leave us alone for too long."

Trying not to smile, I headed back out toward the car. By the time I grabbed the last of the groceries and locked the car, I walked in to find Cooper wrapped around Jackson in a heated embrace. Jackson's hands were kneading Cooper's ass, and they were well on their way to getting naked. "What did I say about sex around the groceries?"

Some days it felt like I was the only adult.

Jackson gave me a wicked grin. It'd only taken seconds for Cooper to talk him into some kind of scheme. "You just said not to have sex over the groceries. You didn't say anything about us taking things to the bedroom."

Setting the groceries down by the table, I snorted. "Same thing."

Jackson's arms wrapped around me pulling me tightly to his chest. "Those two statements are very different. I think Cooper and I need to give you a very detailed example of how *different* they are."

Jackson started walking us out of the kitchen, and I shook my head. "But the groceries?"

Cooper giggled, clearly intent on encouraging Jackson into mischief. "They're not going anywhere."

He was too happy and too relaxed to argue with. I knew we'd eventually have to talk about what had happened, but not yet. No, for now, Jackson and I both just wanted to keep him smiling for as long as possible.

9

JACKSON

"THAT LOOKS wonderful and smells even better." My mother's warm voice had me smiling as I turned to her.

"Thanks. I think they're almost done." Moving the chicken around a little bit more, I closed the lid of the grill. "I'm glad it all worked out. I meant to call you earlier about dinner, but I lost track of time."

After *distracting* both of my boys, and finally putting away the groceries, time had flown by. Eventually, I'd remembered to call about dinner. Thankfully, no one had made any plans. Melissa had some work to do on a new book, so she said she'd be late. But it was almost time for her to get there. The excuse she'd given my parents was that she had errands she needed to run.

"That happens." She glanced toward the garage where Cooper and Sawyer were getting lectures on tools from Dad. "They'll let us know if they want to be rescued, right?"

She sounded slightly skeptical, which made me smile. "They're polite, but they won't let themselves be tortured. I promise." Although their moods were so off today that I wasn't sure if they would say anything. After the incident in the grocery store, we were all a bit on edge.

I wasn't sure if she heard something in my voice or if it was mother's intuition, but she gave me a long look. "Is everything all right? I realize that I'm still getting to know them, but they both seem...stressed, maybe."

I wasn't sure how much to share. Cooper had never been the type to keep everything quiet, though, so I decided to tell her. "We were grocery shopping earlier. We were just having fun and teasing Cooper as we went through the cereal aisle because really, he's like shopping with a five-year-old some days." I had to smile at the memory. He'd been driving Sawyer crazy. Cooper had grabbed that chocolate cereal just to make him nuts.

She smiled, clearly able to picture what shopping with them must look like. "What happened? I'm sure that can't be the reason for their stress."

"We were about ready to leave the aisle when Cooper bumped into someone's cart. I wasn't sure who it was at first, but both of the guys froze. It was like they went from alive and bubbly to mannequins in the space of a second." Standing there, not being able to figure out what caused the change in them had been the longest few seconds of my life.

"It turned out that the older couple he bumped into were his parents. I don't know why they were even there. I'd already asked Sawyer if they lived anywhere close to us because I didn't want to take the chance of making him uncomfortable — of making either of them uncomfortable." There had to have been a reason they were at the store, but until I could figure it out, I wasn't sending Cooper there on his own.

She frowned, shaking her head. "That poor boy. What did they say? I can't imagine it was anything good."

"His mother didn't say a word. She stood there looking shocked and kind of sad. I can't imagine you standing there quietly in the same situation. But then again, I can't imagine you kicking me out."

"Your father is a handful and obstinate on some things, but I can't imagine agreeing with him on anything that would push a child away." She went back to staring at the garage as if she could see through the wall to my sweet boys.

"His dad was a mess. He made some comments about Cooper not having changed and moved them forward. I don't know if things would've been any different if we hadn't been there, but eventually, they would have found out about us."

Mom nodded. "And Cooper isn't the type to hide you."

"I know. He's always been so positive about everything that happened and about knowing they would change someday. I just don't know how this will affect him."

She reached out and squeezed my arm. "What did he say? I can't imagine that you ignored it."

I shrugged and pushed at the guilt that was building. "I tried to bring it up, but he kept changing the subject. All he really said was that he was fine."

She glanced back at the garage like that was something she'd expect to hear from Cooper. "He pretended like nothing had happened and started moving on right away. I think it brought back a lot of sad memories for Sawyer, so he's having a hard time with it, and I wasn't sure what to do. I've never been in that kind of situation. I don't want to screw things up."

"I think the only way you could mess things up would be to continue ignoring it." She finally turned her gaze back to me, giving me a "You're smarter than that" look. "He might honestly be fine. Everybody reacts to trauma differently, but you need to talk to him about it. Something like that could fester and eat away at him and maybe even your relationship."

She shook her head, clearly realizing how that hit me. "But I don't think that would happen. He's made it very clear that you and Sawyer are his family, but that could deteriorate his self-confidence or his ability to feel loved. Parents aren't supposed to walk away from their children like that."

"You're right. It's just hard. I don't want to make him sad." He was my bouncy silly pup, and I didn't want anything to chase the laughter from his eyes.

"They're the ones who started this. You wouldn't be making him sad. You would be helping to heal him. But knowing Cooper, he sees this in his own way. You just won't know what that is until you actually talk about it."

I gave her a smile. "Why are mothers so smart?"

She sighed. "Just some of us. It seems others never learned what that title means. I just can't believe she'd send her child away."

"If she regrets it, she doesn't seem willing to stand up to her husband yet." But there was something about her expression that made me doubt my words. "Maybe I'm judging her too harshly?"

My mother shook her head. "No, you put your children first. Yes, you don't want to raise them to be too entitled or brats, but you don't throw them out for who they are or who they love. And you don't let anyone else do it either."

Her expression took on a harsher tone. "They'd have never found your father's body if he'd tried to do something like that to you. I think I'm smart enough that I wouldn't have gotten caught. And if all else failed, your sister could have helped out. Although, her imagination seems to run to dirtier things than murder."

She smirked when my mouth fell open. "Yes, she thinks she's so clever. Unfortunately, she let your father borrow her car last year when his was in the shop, and she left boxes of books in the trunk. By the look on your face, I'm assuming you know what she writes. That was an education, let me tell you. Your father had all kinds of weird questions."

Oh. My. God.

She was trying to kill me.

"I don't have any idea what you're talking about." I was not getting involved in that.

She chuckled. "If you say so."

It was the ultimate rock and hard place. On one hand, Melissa would kill me and tell all of my secrets if I acknowledged hers. On the other hand, my mother knew her pen name. Survival seemed like the right option, no matter how hard it was. "Melissa works in insurance. What are you talking about?"

Okay, I really was a terrible liar.

Where was Cooper when I needed him?

My little porn star would have been able to handle her easily. Turning back to the grill, I opened the top and checked the chicken. "Everything looks like it's ready. Why don't you go grab them from the garage? Hopefully, you'll rescue them in time, so we won't bring home another birdhouse."

She gave me a knowing look but let me change the subject. "I think you'll be glad to hear that the birdhouse phase might be over. He's looking at learning how to make a dollhouse. Do you know anyone with children?"

I wasn't sure if her expression was because she was hoping I knew someone who would take the project off her hands, or she was hoping I would say we'd have kids. Either way, she was on her own. "No!"

She laughed. "I'll go rescue your young men. But if they've already got birdhouses in their hands, you're out of luck."

There would be no getting out of it. I would be coming home with more birdhouses.

"YOU OKAY?" MELISSA'S VOICE MADE ME JUMP.

She chuckled, but I frowned at her. "I'm fine. How's work?"

I wasn't in the mood to talk about myself, and I hoped she'd let me steer the conversation in another direction. No such luck. "You've been watching your guys like you think they're going to disappear. What's up? Everything all right?"

I knew she was asking to be supportive, but going through this situation again wouldn't make me feel any better. "Just some stuff, but nothing's wrong between us."

"So if it's not about the three of you together, is something wrong with one of the guys? Did Cooper not get the promotion?" She wasn't going to let it drop.

"No, work is fine. It's just some stuff from the past." I took another bite of hamburger, hoping she would get the hint. She probably did, but she was too stubborn to back off.

"What happened?"

For the love of… "Mom knows you're a writer."

Even that conversation would be better than rehashing our trip to the grocery store.

Her mouth fell open, and she glanced back to make sure my mother was still in the house. "What do you mean she knows?"

I snickered, glad she was finally focused on something else. "You left books in the back of the car last year when Dad had it for a couple of days. From what she said, they looked through the books and figured it out."

Her face kept going from white to green as she went through a thousand emotions. It was great — I was going to get to drive her crazy about it, and I hadn't even done it. "Evidently, Mom had to explain some of it to Dad. I don't know if it was the topics or the vocabulary, but he found some a bit confusing."

After everything she'd done to me, I didn't feel guilty about the glee running through me.

"You've got to be kidding!" She couldn't seem to grasp the reality of what I was saying. "You're messing with me."

"No. I have absolutely no reason to tell them or lie. Remember, you've got shit on me. This is all on you."

Thank goodness.

Melissa sat down next to me at the picnic table, trying to compose herself. "They honestly know? What did she say?"

Smiling, I tried to keep my answer vague. "We were talking about somebody that pissed me off. She made a comment that if she needed to kill somebody, she was smart enough not to get caught, but then said if she needed help you'd probably be the one to call. I didn't say anything, but she went on to point out that since you write such dirty stuff, you might not be any help in a murder."

"She totally threw me under the bus. What if you hadn't known?" Then she waved her hand and shook her head like it was ridiculous. "Wait, you're such a bad liar—she would've known right away. But still, she shouldn't have said anything. That's how secrets work."

"In this family?" She and I were pretty good about keeping secrets as long as I didn't have to lie without notice, but when Mom decided she was done letting us hide, she put her foot down. Evidently, she was tired of Melissa hiding her writing.

"She honestly didn't mind? Like, she wasn't upset about what I wrote?" Melissa put one elbow on the table and rested her head in her hand, looking confused but hopeful.

I shrugged. "Not that I could tell. And she said Dad was the one that had the questions. I'm thinking that means she was at least vaguely familiar with some of it."

"What the hell has she been reading lately?" Melissa smiled, looking confused.

"Don't put that image in my head. She's my mother." Some things should remain private. Especially things like what women read.

Melissa chuckled. "At least if she finds out about you guys, she can't claim to be shocked."

Oh, God. "That's not funny. My private life is going to stay private. Got it?" I still had good ammunition on her.

Her eyes danced. "I'm not the one who's going to tattle. We both know Cooper's eventually going to say something."

Okay, she might've had a point there. "Just don't throw me under the bus. I'll drag you with me. She might know about the writing, but I'm sure there's other stuff she doesn't have a clue about."

There was something in her eyes that made me think I'd hit a nerve. "What is it? Are you getting a new job? Finally starting to write full-time? A tattoo? Did you win the lottery? A new guy—"

Yes! I got her. "Who are you dating?"

It had to be good if she was hiding it from Mom.

Her expression clearly said that I was dead meat if I told our parents. I just gave her a casual "I'm not stupid" look and waited. It took her a few seconds to decide what she was going to say. "It's new, but I like him."

That was entirely too vague. "What's wrong with him?"

If he was completely normal, then she wouldn't have bothered hiding him. She shrugged and glanced around the yard to make sure we were still far enough away that no one could hear. Cooper and Sawyer had inhaled their dinner and gone back to the garage with Dad. He was obsessed with showing them all of his power tools, and I think they liked the attention. It was probably good for Cooper.

"There's nothing wrong with him." She paused before continuing. "But she's going to ask where I met him."

I had a feeling we were getting to the good part. Cooper was going to be upset he'd missed the drama. "Where did you meet him?"

Knowing her, it could've been anywhere from a bar to the library. She'd even met one guy at a stoplight, and they'd dated for three months.

She grinned wickedly, clearly thinking it was funny. "Let's just say I was doing some research."

Oh. I probably should've expected that answer.

"What kind of research?" I really didn't want to know, but blackmail material was important.

She shook her head. "Not going to tell you yet. Not until I know if it's going to last."

I thought there was some logic missing in her argument. "So if he ends up being a one-night stand or something, you won't tell me what he's into, but if it's serious and you're going to keep him, then you'll tell me?"

Shouldn't that have been backward?

I hadn't started my relationship with Cooper and Sawyer in the most traditional manner, but if we'd met at the store, or just online, I probably wouldn't have ever told her what they were into. She thought about it for a moment but shook her head. "No, if he's really just a stranger, then protecting his privacy would be important to me. But if he stays around, I don't want to have to watch what I say or tell him to watch what he says. Not around you guys, at least."

I guess she had a point. Knowing that she understood about my relationship with Cooper and Sawyer made it easier. "Would you tell Mom and Dad?"

"No! It's just weird."

So, me knowing wasn't weird, but them knowing was?

"I guess that makes sense." But it really didn't.

Not that I was going to argue with her about it. It wouldn't be worth the headache. "I don't have to hide this from Cooper and Sawyer, do I?"

That wasn't really how our life worked. Thankfully, she shook her head. "No, just make sure they know not to say anything."

"Got it." Before the conversation could continue, the boys

came out of the garage. They were all smiles and laughter, carrying pieces of wood.

Cooper started almost skipping across the yard when he saw me, leaving Sawyer to walk slower. "Look! It's going to be mine. I did it!"

I knew I was supposed to be impressed, so I smiled and nodded, but it wasn't enough information. "You cut the pieces?"

Cooper shoved the wood into my hands, smiling like he just passed me a new baby. "It's going to be fabulous. Your dad said that I can paint it whatever color I want."

For goodness' sake. Another fucking birdhouse. "I know it's going to turn out fabulous. It looks like it's already coming together great."

There wasn't anything I could really visualize from several rectangular pieces of wood, but the cuts were straight and it wasn't lopsided, so that automatically made it better than some of my dad's first tries.

He beamed and wiggled his fingers at me. "And I still have my fingers." But he frowned, looking down at one. "I think I have a splinter. That doesn't count as an injury, though. That's just a hazard of the job."

I wasn't going to smile.

I wasn't going to laugh.

"I'm glad you still have all your fingers. What color are you going to paint it?" With my Cooper, there was no way to guess.

Sawyer came up with his wood to stand beside me. He leaned into my shoulder, smiling. "He told your dad he was going to paint it pink. But I think that was just to mess with him."

Cooper looked slightly guilty but grinned even wider. "Maybe. But we have to go to the store this week and look at paint colors. I want it to be fabulous."

What color was fabulous?

"Of course, we just have to figure out when we can all go."

Sawyer shook his head. "Oh no, I'm just going to use a dark stain that your dad already has. You guys have fun picking out colors."

I loved doing things with Cooper, and watching him bounce through the paint section sounded...interesting. Smiling, I nodded. "That's fine. I think they're both going to turn out wonderfully."

"We've got to come back next week and work on them some more." Cooper's infectious smile made me want to pull him into my arms. He was so cute and so excited.

"Sure, we'll work out the details later this week." Even if barbecuing wouldn't work, there was probably time over the weekend that we could all get together.

"And we have to figure out a place to put it." Cooper's eyes sparkled, and I knew part of his enjoyment was knowing my opinion on the birdhouses.

But I wouldn't argue with anything that brought a smile to his face. No, with as much as he had going on, and all the things that were worrying him, if something made him happy, we'd do it. But my mother's words were still rolling around in the back of my head.

I knew she was right, but I wasn't looking forward to the conversation. I loved my boys desperately and bringing up anything that would hurt them seemed wrong. Even if Cooper was as okay as he seemed, Sawyer and I weren't. And we wouldn't be until we'd had a chance to talk to him.

Pulling my boys into my arms, I gave them both chaste kisses on the forehead. "I love you."

They both snuggled in, smiling. I loved them enough to bring home extra birdhouses. That should have said more than anything how much they meant to me.

10

COOPER

"A POOL...A hot tub...maybe. No, the hot tub...all those jets and bubbles..." I stretched out on the bed, staring up at the ceiling. Having the house all to myself was always weird. But sometimes it was nice. Like when I could stretch out on the bed naked and just relax. Being able to play with myself would have made it better, but Jackson had a class, and I wouldn't interrupt him just to ask if I could orgasm. Not this time, at least.

"Wait. There isn't enough privacy in the backyard for a hot tub." Talking him into a hot tub would be one thing—if I had to add in a privacy fence and stuff to keep everyone from seeing him naked, that wouldn't work.

I was good, but I wasn't a miracle worker.

"But it would be so perfect." Instead of lying on the bed talking to myself, I could have been floating in the hot tub talking to myself.

It wasn't like I had nothing to do. I just didn't feel like doing it.

Normally, that wouldn't have been a problem, but I'd told Jackson and Sawyer earlier about my big plans for the day. So doing nothing wasn't really an option. They'd just start to worry more and ask if I was okay again. I was fine; that wasn't the problem. I was nervous and lazy. That was nothing out of the ordinary. But they wouldn't believe it.

I was going to have to sit down with them and make them talk about their feelings. They kept everything too bottled up and had been slightly nuts since the grocery store. At first, I'd thought they'd needed time to deal with things, but that wasn't working. No, it was a wound that festered, not something that would clear up on its own.

"Time to rip off the Band-Aid." Wait…if it had festered, it probably needed something better than a Band-Aid. I might have to work on that analogy.

"Whatever I'm ripping off, it's time." That didn't sound quite as good, but it would have to work. They were driving me crazy.

Maybe I was being too hard on them. I could understand why they were worried. For Sawyer, it was probably bringing up bad memories of the night that I'd left. He felt everything so strongly, and I knew those first few weeks had been hard on him.

For Jackson, it was probably very confusing. His own family was funny and understanding. I couldn't imagine them pushing him away. Jackson just couldn't relate to the idea that some people didn't embrace change or ideas that were different very well.

Yeah, we were going to have to talk. My worrier and my master both needed someone to take care of them.

But that would have to wait until they got home and I functioned. "Okay, shower first and then coffee. After that, I'll work on my to-do list."

Rolling over, I grabbed my phone off the nightstand to see what time it was. Not late enough. I glanced down at my erection. "You're just going to have to wait."

Unfortunately.

I didn't hurry to get off the bed, but eventually, I was standing. Getting a shower didn't take that long, especially when I had to skip all the fun parts of getting wet and naked. Once I was out and reasonably dry, I went back into the bedroom and started digging around in my drawers. With customers over at the training building all day, being naked wasn't a good idea.

"A privacy fence would fix a lot of that, though. Maybe not enough that we could walk around naked but...oh, I could run around the yard as my pup. That would be perfect." Yes, we'd begin with the fence and work our way to the hot tub.

I pulled a pair of basketball shorts on and headed for the kitchen. Jackson said I had to wear clothes, but he hadn't said anything about underwear. The coffee looked like it'd been sitting for too long, so I threw out the last of it and made a new pot. When the delicious aroma was working its way through the kitchen, I looked around for something to eat.

When I had days off, most of the time I would get up with them and have breakfast. Jackson's schedule was usually flexible enough that we would sit around talking over coffee quite a while after Sawyer left. But he'd gone in early to rearrange some things, and I had a vague memory of him talking about paperwork.

He really needed an accountant.

I was better with people than math. He wasn't so hot with math either, but puppies were where Master succeeded fabulously. Jackson had said we could probably have time later if I wanted it. Which was a silly question—I couldn't imagine not wanting it. And as stressed as Sawyer had been the last couple of days, it probably would be good for him as well. "Time for everybody to relax and me to have fun."

As I dug out some leftover Chinese to reheat, I grinned. "Chase the ball...I'm going to get orgasms....It's going to be great."

And it was going to be orgasms with an *J*. If I had to wait this morning, we would need to have a lot of fun to make up for it. "Oh yes, lots of fun for making me wait."

Jackson was going to love my logic.

When my coffee was ready and my leftover Chinese food was hot, I sat down at the table and played with my phone. It wasn't as good as cuddling up with Jackson over coffee, but it would have to work. I should have been working on my to-do list, but I figured since I was out of bed, it would count toward me functioning for a while.

It wasn't that I didn't want to do it. It was just so overwhelming.

As far as the first step for college went, setting up my online account and figuring out how the blackboard and email systems worked wasn't that hard. It just made it very real. Everything else from filling out the initial paperwork to picking out classes had been theoretical.

It was like one of those discussions about what someone would be when they grew up. What they would do if they won the lottery. Only now, I had to follow through with everything. I kept hearing Sawyer's voice in my head talking about how smart I was, but there was a big difference between high school and college.

At least, that was what everyone used to say.

High school academics hadn't been that hard. It had been the social things and figuring out who I was that had been difficult. Classes had been about paying attention and taking notes and doing homework. It had felt very straightforward and logical.

College couldn't be any different. Could it?

"So what have you been up to?" Jackson's voice made

me jump, but it was the arms that wrapped around me that made me squeal.

He chuckled and leaned down to kiss my cheek. "I'm sorry. I thought you heard me."

I shook my head. "No, I think you can tell by my reaction that I didn't." I turned my face and stuck out my tongue at him. "You did that on purpose."

He shrugged, looking slightly guilty. "Possibly. But you were dancing around and playing the music so loud that I couldn't resist the temptation. If you want me to behave, you shouldn't be running around the house nearly naked."

I barked out a laugh. "I've got shorts on."

As I turned in his arms, his hands moved down my back to cup my ass. He gave both cheeks a squeeze and grinned. "But you don't have a shirt on and as far as I can tell, there is nothing restraining your sexy hard-on, so it counts."

"You're the reason for this"—I swung my hips, letting my erection grind against his body—"problem, so you can't complain."

"I'm not complaining, pup. You're beautiful." He tightened his grip and kissed my forehead. "But I kind of expected to come in and find you on the computer. Did you get everything done?"

I loved how he was trying to be subtle and supportive, but the way he glanced around the kitchen gave him away. "I've been busy."

That wasn't a lie.

I'd vacuumed the house.

I'd mopped the kitchen.

I dusted everything. Because, come on, the feather duster was fun.

I just hadn't exactly gotten to the school stuff.

Jackson, clearly understanding my creative truth-telling,

didn't ask a stupid question like why I'd cleaned the house. "What was next on your list?"

I didn't have to lie that time or come up with a creative version of the truth. "I was going to get another cup of coffee and see if there was any cheesecake left. It somehow seems to have disappeared."

It was Jackson's turn to look guilty. "I don't know what happened. A piece here, a little piece there, then it was gone. I think I had some help, though."

I shook my head like I was sad and gave him an innocent look. "It has to be Sawyer. He's sneaky like that."

Jackson shrugged and nodded. "I can see that. He's clearly the type to sneak bites when everyone else isn't home, or say he's taking lunch to work when he really just grabbed a banana and a huge slice of cheesecake."

Oops.

I was going to have to sneak smaller pieces next time.

"Yep, we'll have to watch him better in the future."

A grin broke out on his face, and his eyes sparkled. "I think I can guarantee, I'll keep a closer watch on him. In fact, I might just keep a closer watch on both of you. Because I have a feeling there's something we need to talk about."

Cuddling closer to Jackson, I let my cock rub against his hip. I wasn't going to seduce him to get out of talking, but if he distracted us first, then it wouldn't be my fault.

Jackson chuckled, and one hand reached down to smack my ass. "No distracting me, pup. You've cleaned most of the house. You've done everyone's chores, including your own. It's almost frightening."

I sighed. "I was supposed to be getting everything with the university set up online. At first, I was distracted by regular things. But once I was dressed and functioning, I still couldn't do it."

Jackson's arms tightened around me, and I felt him press a kiss to the top of my head. "It's a big change for you."

He didn't ask any questions or press for answers. That made it even harder to stay silent. "What if it's not like high school? What if it's harder and just doesn't work? I'm not saying I think I'm dumb. It's just...huge."

"You're right."

That wasn't what I'd been expecting him to say. But it made me feel less crazy. "I know. I'm always right."

Jackson chuckled, and his hand came up to caress my head. "This is a *big* change. It would be for anyone. And in this case, everything that happened makes it more important. You already started planning this once, and everything got ripped away from you."

I hadn't thought of it like that. "Sawyer likes to say that I got good grades in high school, and he's right. He's not just saying that. I graduated with one of the highest GPAs in our graduating class. I didn't quite ace the SAT, but I did really well on that too. I probably could have gotten academic scholarships, but my parents didn't think it was important. So I never got around to filling out the paperwork."

I could hear the smile in Jackson's voice. "Sawyer loves to brag about you. He's so proud of everything you accomplished. You probably could have gotten some fabulous scholarships."

"I didn't care about scholarships or even money. It wasn't something I ever thought about. Looking back, it was probably a status thing for them. Being able to say they paid for my college outright would have made them feel more superior."

"For some people, that kind of thing is important."

"It wasn't for me. I saw college as a chance to escape and figure out who I was. I always knew there were different parts of me inside that wanted to get out. When I found the puppy play online, I knew I'd found a big part of it. I never planned on telling them. Not because I was ashamed of it but because it was private."

"I can understand that. There are some things you just don't want to tell your parents."

"Like the fact that you want a tail and to run around chasing a tennis ball because it's fun and turns you on."

Jackson snorted. "Or that you get turned on by watching a guy with a tail crawl around chasing a tennis ball."

I giggled. "Yeah, that too."

"Or the fact that you want to bend your boyfriend over your lap, so you can spank his bottom."

"Or the fact that you want to do it with two boyfriends."

Jackson's body shook with silent laughter. "Yes, although that conversation would go over a lot easier now than it might have in the past."

Now I was the one laughing. "I can't believe she left the books in the car."

"She was always so good at being devious in the past. Part of me thinks she wanted to get caught."

I nodded against his chest. "At least subconsciously. I'm just glad your parents were accepting."

I felt his body shift, and I pictured him nodding, but I didn't move. I was too comfortable. "I don't even want to know what kind of questions my father had."

"That would be the best conversation ever." Giggling, I could almost see it in my head. Jackson's dad was so funny with his serious but endearing obsessions—I knew it had to have been priceless.

"That's terrible. I don't ever want to hear my parents discussing sex. Especially kinky sex." Jackson shuddered and had the same sound in his voice as when we'd teased him in the grocery store. He was so cute.

"Okay, I won't torture you by telling you all the crazy things he probably doesn't know about kinky sex."

"Cooper!"

Laughing, I wrapped my arms around him. "I'll be good."

"I think the only way you'll be good is if I keep you occupied. How about we go lie down on the bed and you show me the site? We'll do it together." Jackson pressed another kiss to my head, and his hand moved down my back in slow strokes.

"What about work? I remember you saying that you didn't have any classes this afternoon, but there's probably paperwork or cleaning that needs to be done." His schedule was flexible sometimes, but I didn't want him to miss work just because I was nervous.

"I didn't make any plans for this afternoon. I thought if you were done, we'd go get tested. I think this is more important, though."

I wasn't sure about that. "The website will wait."

I'd rather get the testing out of the way, so I could really feel him inside me instead of doing school stuff. Jackson chuckled. "I think this is more important. It's not that late. We have time for both."

Glancing at the clock, I realized he was right. "Have you eaten lunch yet? I don't remember if you took a sandwich out there or not."

Pulling back from Jackson, I looked up at him. He shook his head. "I'll make one now, and then we'll go lie down. You can show me what you know, and we'll look over the rest together. I'm not going to let you distract me, though. Got it?" The master in him flared in his eyes, and I knew he was serious. It made me feel safer, and for some reason, more confident.

"Yes, Master." Stretching up, I gave him a tender kiss. "Just don't make a mess in the kitchen. I've spent all morning cleaning it. I've got to be done with cleaning for the next couple of weeks."

Jackson laughed and his eyes danced with pleasure. "Oh no, it doesn't count when you do everyone else's chores."

"Hey, it does too."

"How about we wait and see what Sawyer says? He also might find the fact that you ate the last of the cheesecake interesting."

"That's blackmail."

He nodded, thoroughly enjoying himself. "Yes, I learned it from you, pup."

Damn. It was hard to argue with that.

11

SAWYER

"MR. DUNHAM, DO YOU HAVE A MOMENT?" The five seconds it took for him to look up from his desk were some of the longest of my life.

It had taken me more time than I'd planned to talk to him about the dinner, but it wasn't just fear that'd held me back. Honestly, I wasn't sure I had the right words to explain why I was frustrated. I hoped what I had to say would make sense and not backfire.

He glanced up, smiling, and set his paperwork down. "Sawyer, of course. This is actually good timing. I was going to see if I could find you before you left for the day."

I quickly did a mental review of everything on my to-do list that day, but I couldn't think of anything he would have wanted to talk to me about. Pushing that aside for the moment, I stepped into his office. The building was quickly emptying out, so I didn't bother closing the door. There would be plenty of privacy, even if the conversation went badly.

"I'd like to talk to you about dinner the other night." Finding the words was hard. I'd been practicing it for days, but nothing sounded right. I volleyed between too passive and too confrontational. I didn't want him to think I was angry, but I also didn't want him to brush it off.

However, before I could continue, he sighed and leaned back in his chair. "Lee said I owed you an apology."

That was unexpected.

"Sir?" I wasn't sure where he was starting to take the conversation.

Luckily, I didn't have to guess. "Evidently, my wanting to make them comfortable may have been misconstrued."

He looked a little bit like a child who'd been sent to apologize. It was clear he didn't quite get what he'd done wrong, but he seemed to understand it hadn't worked out the way he'd intended. "We don't exactly live in a small town, but there aren't that many companies like ours in the area. So really, the gossip mill between owners and staff of the different companies works like a small town."

He had a point, so I couldn't argue with what he'd said so far. That didn't mean I knew what was going on, though. I didn't have to guess, however, because his odd explanation kept going. "I'd heard from several people that some of the meetings hadn't gone well. The usual contractors they'd partnered with in the past were too small to handle the scale of the new development. Unfortunately, looking for new contractors hasn't been easy. Several people who I spoke with didn't understand why the meetings had gone so badly, so I may have overreacted in trying not to offend."

Yes, I could picture Lee lecturing him as soon as she'd realized what he'd done. It had some of the last bits of frustration fading, and I tried not to smile. "I understand your thoughts on the situation."

Suddenly I wished I had Cooper's ease with talking to people. He wouldn't have had any issue taking Mr. Dunham to task. "If you'd have explained the situation beforehand, I may have even agreed with you."

The people I worked with were more comfortable with plants and drawings than customers sometimes. "However, I should have been given some warning. Everyone was at a loss over my reason for being there, and it made things unnecessarily awkward."

Mr. Dunham cocked his head, looking slightly confused. Thinking back over what I'd said, I wasn't sure where I'd lost him. He sat up in his chair and rested his arms on his desk. "What do you mean? I thought Ralph told you about the meeting."

I shook my head. "No, his daughter had the flu last week, and his wife was at a conference. He had most of that week off, remember?"

What was he supposed to have talked to me about?

"Mitch said you needed me at the dinner and then made some vague comments about how big it was going to be, but that it was in the middle of nowhere. That's it." There'd also been some vague comments about me helping them fit in, which hadn't helped the confusion any.

Mr. Dunham gave a bark of laughter, but it was filled with more frustration than happiness. "Oh God, that must have seemed even worse."

He leaned back again in his chair, mumbling something about someone killing him. He actually looked apologetic. "No, Ralph was supposed to have talked to you about the project before we went. Not the specifics, because we didn't have much to go on, but we'd talked about you working on the team who would handle the design."

They'd what?

My confusion, and probably shock, made him smile. "It's going to turn out to be one of the biggest we've ever done. The scale of the development is immense. We have the manpower, but everyone else's plate is pretty full."

He paused, letting that sink in before he continued. "We talked about bringing you on in a different role for this one. It wouldn't necessarily be a traditional raise, but there would be some additional compensation for the extra work." That sounded enough like a raise that I wasn't going to complain.

"Again, I'm sorry. He was supposed to have talked to you last week about the new role. I didn't realize he was out for that many days. With everything going on, it must have slipped his mind. Yes, I'll admit that your relationship made things easier." I was glad he didn't skip that part, but I still wasn't sure how he'd felt about the situation.

"I wanted them to see that we didn't have an issue with their marriage. But without your hard work and good designs to back it up, we would never have included you. And Lee said I needed to make this clear—if all we needed was someone in a non-heterosexual relationship, then there were other members of the staff I could have invited. But I'm not supposed to say names, because evidently, that would be inappropriate too."

Their conversation must have been a doozy.

"Yes, some discretion would be a good idea in that situation." I was pretty much the guy who kept his head down and didn't pay attention to a lot of the social dynamics going on at work, so I wasn't sure who he was talking about.

There had been a variety of single people as well as people in established relationships at the barbecue, but it would have never occurred to me to ask someone about who they were dating. It was work, not a bar where I was trying to pick up people.

"That clears up a few things. Thank you."

I was going to get a promotion. Kind of. "I think working on the project would be very interesting. From the little comments he made at dinner, it's going to be challenging."

Just the number of different areas in the developments would make it a daunting task. Add in the variety of uses the spaces would have and the diverse feel that each section of the development would need, and it would be difficult.

Sitting up straighter, he smiled and looked relieved. "Good. I'm glad that's settled. We'll go into more details at the meeting on Friday. I haven't announced it yet officially, but I signed the contract earlier today."

"What meeting?" We were going to have to figure out a way to make sure I wasn't the last to know everything. "And congratulations."

"Oh, I think I'm going to have to have a conversation with Ralph about keeping you in the loop. I apologize."

"He wasn't here today. He caught his daughter's flu." He'd left early the previous day, looking terrible. We'd all made it very clear that he wasn't to come back until he was no longer contagious.

"Oh, that's right." My boss glanced down at his desk like he'd lost something. "I need to make a note to have someone else keep you up-to-date. At least until everything settles down for Ralph. If I'm remembering correctly, last year around this time they all came down with some kind of sinus infection or head cold. Didn't he end up giving that to half the office?"

I laughed. "Yes, that's why we sent him home early yesterday. No one wants a repeat of that disaster."

He nodded distractedly. "Yes, that's what I thought. Okay, so we're going to keep you more informed. And I really am sorry about that. But at the meeting on Friday, we'll go over more of the details and the scale of the project. The rest of the team who'll be heading up the project are meeting at two o'clock, so I want you there. Then we'll start talking about the feel and themes and plan it out from there."

It wasn't technically a promotion, but that was what it boiled down to. At least for this one, I was going to be able to give my input and actually help plan the design. I was having a hard time wrapping my brain around it.

"Sounds good. It should be interesting." That was a huge understatement and probably something I'd said too many times already, but I didn't want to look overeager and too excited.

"I agree." He looked back down at his desk. "All right, I think I have everything set for the day."

"Yes, and I need to head out as well." Not that I was going to mention where I was stopping on the way home. After the excited text that I'd gotten from Cooper, I wasn't going to be the one to hold us back.

As I walked out of his office, Mr. Dunham spoke again. "And please, I know I've said this before, but call me Howard."

It hadn't felt right before, but he had a point now. Nodding, I smiled. "Howard. Have a good evening."

He smiled like I'd made his day. For a moment, I felt like I was sitting at the cool table and he was just excited to be invited in. As I headed toward the front of the building, I looked at the situation from a little bit of a different perspective, and I wished I hadn't put off the conversation as long as I had. Cooper was going to have a field day with the I-told-you-sos.

"DID YOU DO IT?" COOPER NEARLY TACKLED ME AS I OPENED the door.

Laughing, I nodded. I'd thought about teasing him and telling him I had to work late. His excitement was too infectious, however. "Yes, just like I said I would."

He grinned ear to ear and wiggled even closer, pressing his erection against me. "Just a couple of days and then no more condoms with Jackson."

I was as enthusiastic as Cooper but in my own way. The idea of making love to Jackson without a condom was incredible. I didn't remember it being a big decision with Cooper, but we'd been in a different place in our relationship. It'd been a logical next step, not a significant milestone in our life.

It was different with Jackson.

We both saw it, so I didn't feel guilty about it. It was letting Jackson claim us in a way. He wasn't the type to go all caveman and get ridiculously possessive. And no matter what goofy role-play scenarios he enacted with Cooper, our past relationships had never bothered him. So I didn't know why it was special. I wasn't going to let myself overanalyze it, though. I was going to take a page from Cooper's playbook and just accept what I liked and how I felt about it.

I wanted my master to mark me as his, and there was nothing wrong with that.

"I bet you thought about all kinds of wicked things you want him to do to you." With the way Cooper's mind worked, he'd most likely thought of a thousand sexy options.

Cooper sighed dramatically, nodding. "Oh yes, I think I'm going to make a list, so I don't forget any." With anyone else, I would have thought they were teasing, but knowing Cooper, he was serious. It would probably end up on the refrigerator, where he'd get to check dirty fantasies off his list.

"Coop, you're nuts, but I love you."

He smirked and gave me a knowing look. "Of course you love me. I'm fabulous. And you can't pretend you don't have a naughty list too."

I wasn't planning on denying it, but I also wasn't going to write it down like some kind of erotic to-do list. "My imagination isn't as good as yours."

"Bullshit. Your imagination is just quieter. Mine yells everything out so loud that I have to share." He leaned in and gave me a heated kiss. Pulling back, he dropped his voice to a sexy whisper. "I bet you can't wait to hear some of the things on my list."

He was right, and he knew it. But before I could respond, Jackson walked into the kitchen. "What are you up to, nut? It sounds like you're getting into trouble."

I nodded. "He's trying to seduce me. Even though you told him not to play with himself, he is rubbing his cock against me. He's also trying to tempt me with his dirty fantasies." I grinned as Cooper pouted.

He couldn't decide if he was frustrated that I'd shoved him under the bus or glad I'd given Jackson the idea that he needed to be punished. Indecision was clear on his face, and I could almost see the questions flying through his mind.

Should he fess up and admit he'd been naughty?

Would denying it and claiming to be good get a reward?

Did he want a spanking or a more traditional reward?

A spanking.

Cooper turned in my arms but stayed leaning against me and gave Jackson a sexy look. "I'm sorry, Master. I was just so excited. I forgot to be good because Sawyer asked me if I'd been thinking of dirty fantasies. It really is all his fault."

Jackson was trying not to grin, but I didn't appreciate being thrown under the bus when he'd started it. "Hey, you jumped on me as soon as I walked in the door, wiggling and rubbing your dick against me. I was being good and thinking about what to make for dinner before you threw yourself at me."

Ha. If anyone was going to get a reward for being good, it was me.

Besides, Cooper liked getting punished just as much as getting rewarded.

Jackson smiled and shook his head as he walked over to us. Wrapping his arms around us both, he tugged us close. I got a tender, lingering kiss welcoming me home, and Cooper got a smack to his ass. "I think I can figure out who was probably naughty."

Cooper huffed, but it was impossible to hide the smile that was showing through.

He gave Cooper a knowing look before turning to me. "Did you have anything in mind? The afternoon was busier than I thought, and I forgot to lay the chicken out."

"I thought you worked this morning." Depending on the paperwork and things that came up, however, he'd sometimes work a lot longer than planned.

Jackson nodded. "Yes, but then Cooper and I got distracted browsing around the school website before we went to get tested."

"See, he is distracting everyone today."

Jackson chuckled, and Cooper wiggled excitedly. "You're right. I think we might need to remind him how to be good."

That sounded like a promising evening. But before I could say anything, my stomach growled. Cooper giggled, and Jackson leaned in to give me a kiss on the forehead. "Dinner before punishments. What do you guys want to do? Should we go out?"

I considered Jackson's question for a moment, but all I really wanted to do was relax. "How about we just order pizza and stay here?"

Cooper bounced excitedly. "Yes, there's a new episode of that sci-fi show on."

It actually held his attention long enough that Jackson and I got to relax, so I nodded. "That sounds like a good evening to me."

I turned my attention back to Jackson. "What do you think?"

"Sounds perfect. You go get comfortable and I'll call." As he stepped away, he gave Cooper a stern look. "No distracting him. You're going to have to wait until you're showing me you can be good, and I haven't decided about Sawyer yet. So you have to behave."

Not knowing what would happen or if I'd get to come shouldn't have been that exciting. Just seconds before, all I'd wanted to do was curl up on the couch with them, but with that one sentence, my thoughts took a sexier turn, and I couldn't wait for dinner to be over.

I had a feeling it was going to be an interesting evening.

12

JACKSON

I WOKE up to see the boys sprawled across the bed. It was still early for a Saturday, but there was too much on my mind to sleep in. Sawyer was pressed against my side, curled into me like he hadn't moved all night. Cooper, on the other hand, took up half the bed and had somehow ended up completely upside down.

He was as wiggly in his sleep as he was when he was awake. I couldn't help but think that the stress of the past week or so hadn't made things any easier. I thought we might have handled some of the concerns he had about college, but we still hadn't sat down and had a good conversation about his parents. That was partly my fault, but the rest was just because he was Cooper. When I pinned him down long enough to have a conversation, we either went completely off track or got deliciously distracted.

It was time to stop running from the discussion and remind all of us, me included, why they called me Master.

Rolling over toward Cooper, I draped one arm over his legs and started tickling his feet with the other. When he began to writhe and groan, I pinned his legs to the bed. I had no desire to end up with a black eye from a squirming Cooper. It would end up being a story that got completely out of hand like the dildo bruise.

His little noises and movements had Sawyer lifting his head to see what I was doing. He gave a laugh and wrapped himself around me while I continued to torment Cooper's feet. Eventually, Cooper's eyes opened, but instead of complaining, he lifted his hips and wiggled his butt. "I have better things for you to tickle if you want to play."

I gave the tempting skin a smack that echoed through the quiet bedroom. Cooper moaned and offered it up even more. I chuckled but shook my head. "Come up here. I want to talk to you first. Then see about tickling your *better things*."

He giggled and turned around as I released his legs. "I'll be right back."

He scrambled off the bed, nearly falling when he got stuck in the sheet. He managed to catch himself at the last minute but landed with a thud that had Sawyer and me both concerned. "I will not be a happy master if you break yourself."

He grinned and shrugged before making a naked dash to the bathroom. He called out as the door closed, "There's some kind of 'you break it, you bought' joke in there, but I haven't had any caffeine. I'll figure out why it's funny later."

Sawyer groaned, and I found him smiling as I rolled back over. He glanced toward the bathroom and shook his head. "He's going to be figuring out that joke all morning. We'll get a thousand variations, but none of them will actually be funny."

"But he knows that too, and that's why it's going to be funny." My boys knew almost everything about each other, but that didn't seem to have faded the sparkle in their relationship. No, it'd just made it more special and more precious.

Sawyer leaned in and gave me a kiss. "I'll be right back." As he started to climb out of the bed with more grace than Cooper had shown, he gave me a solemn look. "Time to talk about his parents?"

I nodded. "Yes—I was hoping that he would bring it up, but since he hasn't, I think it's time I did."

I wasn't sure what Sawyer thought of it, because he was quiet for a long moment. Finally, he nodded slowly. "I think it would be easier for me to understand his reaction if I wasn't so close to it. But since I basically lived through it with him, it's coloring how I see it."

I sat up and moved closer to the side of the bed. Wrapping my arms around Sawyer, I gave him another quick kiss. "That's understandable. You're not a mind reader. Even if ninety-nine percent of the time you know exactly what he's going to do, you don't have to feel bad for the other one percent. And I'd be shocked if it didn't upset you. You're closer than most people who've been married for years, and anything that might upset Cooper is going to affect you. That's why we're going to talk it out. Once we know how he feels, then we can figure out a way to handle it."

Sawyer nodded, and some of the stress he was holding in faded, but I knew the rest of it wouldn't go away until we'd all had a chance to talk. Since I was feeling the same way, I could completely relate. Before Sawyer could say anything else, Cooper came bounding out of the bathroom. He ran across the room and jumped onto the bed, laughing and smiling.

Sawyer grinned and shook his head but got off the bed and headed for the bathroom. "Someone is a little attention whore this morning."

Cooper jumped to his knees and waved his hand like a good little student in class. "Me! Me!"

Laughing at both of their antics, I reached out and wrapped my arms around him, pulling him down to the mattress. "You stay right here. I'll be right back."

He pretended to freeze on the mattress as I got off the bed

and went to the guest bathroom. By the time I returned, they were both sitting on the bed, Cooper trying his best to look innocent and Sawyer clearly ready to tattle.

They were so funny.

Standing at the end of the bed, I folded my arms and gave Cooper a stern look. It would have looked ridiculous if I was naked, so I was glad I'd put on cotton sleep pants the night before. "Cooper, what did you do?"

His face looked sweet and blameless, but his naked body and clearer erection took his innocent look in another direction. He shrugged and shook his head, obviously deciding to play dumb. "I don't know what he's talking about."

Sawyer snorted, and I tried not to chuckle. "Well, considering the fact that he hasn't said anything yet, I think you've probably been up to something."

Sawyer nodded and gave Cooper a frustrated look. The boxer shorts he was wearing were less distracting, but his erection was still clearly outlined. "He asked for kisses when I got back into bed. So I cuddled close, and we kissed. But before long, he was trying to kiss down my chest and said he wanted to kiss my *interesting places*."

Cooper giggled.

I gave him a frown that probably wasn't believable in the least and climbed onto the bed. "Naughty boy. I think we're going to have to punish you later."

Cooper squirmed, and his cock jerked. "But no spankings for you this time. I think we need to do something else to help you remember to be good."

He couldn't seem to decide if he wanted to cheer or pout. He'd been looking forward to a spanking and now wasn't sure what I had in mind. Trying to look slightly contrite, he nodded. "Yes, Master. I'm sorry."

He was just sorry he wasn't going to get a spanking.

"I told you that you should've behaved." Sawyer was trying

to tease him, but I could see the worry starting to show in his eyes.

Climbing up from the end of the bed, I settled between the two of them and leaned back on the pillows. They both snuggled close. Sawyer was resting his head on my chest, and Cooper had his on my shoulder with one leg draped over mine.

Before I could say anything, Cooper looked up at me. "You guys have been tense lately. Do you want to talk about what happened in the grocery store? I know it upset you."

He left us both speechless.

Finally, Sawyer chuckled. "That was kind of the speech we were going to give you."

Cooper looked at us like we were ridiculous. "I'm not the one who's all tense and worried. That's you two."

I tried to resist the urge to smile, but it was almost impossible. I finally gave in and kissed his forehead. "We've been worried because we didn't know how you were handling it. You've been quiet about the whole situation, and we've been waiting for you to let us know you needed to talk about it, but the silence is making it worse for us."

He cocked his head like I'd said something curious. "I'm never silent."

Sawyer barked out a laugh.

Cooper and I gave him a "Can't you behave?" look, but he shrugged. "Sorry, but that was funny."

Okay, so it was funny, but that wasn't the point. Turning my attention back to Cooper, I nodded. "I didn't mean silent in general, I meant you were very quiet about what happened."

He nodded, seemingly agreeing with the statement. "What did you need me to talk about?"

I felt like we were talking in circles around the conversation. It was almost like we were speaking two different languages. "Let's start with how it made you feel."

He thought about it for a moment. I didn't know if it was

because it was difficult to articulate or if he wasn't sure. "Slightly impatient, I guess."

Okay, I was stumped.

I turned to Sawyer to see if he could translate, but he simply shrugged. Seeing that it was left up to me, I tried to figure out a logical response. "Impatient about what?"

His answer was quicker that time. "That it's taking him so long to realize he's wrong. I guess we're about halfway there, but I thought we'd be closer to seventy-five percent at this point."

Hmm. "So one hundred percent would mean that he realized he was wrong and was ready to make amends?"

Cooper nodded and looked at me like he hoped I was feeling better. I was more confused than anything else. "How do you know he is about halfway there?"

"Well, there were no obscenities this time, and he was a lot calmer. He's one of those guys who stays worked up for a long time. He'll get there eventually, though." His firm conviction made me smile.

"So you weren't upset?"

"No, mostly just confused. Do you think they moved? They used to live on the other side of town. I hope they got a good deal on the house. It needed some renovations, and that would have affected the value. He's not really handy, though, and probably refused to hire someone to fix it. Hopefully, Mom got it all worked out."

Every time I thought I understood him, something would come out that made me sit back and look at him again. "They didn't have that much in their cart, so I was thinking they were just there to grab a few things because of some kind of social commitment."

Cooper nodded. "Yeah, that's what I was thinking. It makes more sense than moving. My mom loves her kitchen."

Sawyer's body sank into mine, and I could almost feel the

stress leaving his body. "I'm still completely pissed at your parents."

Cooper gave him a soft smile and stretched over me to kiss him. "Because you love me. It's okay. It'll all work out, eventually. You'll see."

"How are you so sure?" I knew he saw the good in everyone and in every situation, but I didn't understand how his conviction was so strong.

He shrugged. "I don't know how to explain it. I know it's going to be fine. Sometimes you just have to be patient with people."

I had a bit too much of my mother in me for that level of understanding. I felt slightly guilty, but I was in her camp. We'd just bury the bodies and worry about the details later.

Sawyer, on the other hand, wanted more details now. "What happens if they get to that point but can't find you?"

Cooper seemed to think that was ridiculous. "Of course they could find me."

Sawyer seemed to be fighting the urge to roll his eyes. "You aren't just going to magically run into them in the grocery store every year."

Cooper gave us another confused look. "My mother friended me on Facebook two years ago. She'll message me when they're ready."

We looked at him again in shock.

He continued, not bothered by our twin expressions. "Her profile's mainly blank. But last year on my birthday, when you posted that message on my wall, she liked it. I think that's making good progress."

I couldn't decide if I wanted to squeeze him and tell him how much I loved him or shake him. "I love you, Cooper. But how about you share some of this with us next time?"

He nodded, but his expression said I was being ridiculous. "I would have said it if someone had asked. You were both just so upset, I didn't want to bring it up. I don't like seeing you sad."

That made me smile, and I pulled him close for a kiss. As he pulled away, I smiled at him and reached up to run my hands through his hair. "I can understand that. Thank you for thinking of us."

As Cooper relaxed back onto me and sighed, I glanced over at Sawyer. I wasn't the only one who'd been surprised by that conversation. He was shaking his head and looking at Cooper like he was an alien who was sexy but confusing as hell.

My life would never be boring with them in it. I smiled at Sawyer and leaned over to give him a kiss. "Love you."

"Because I'm not crazy and I make sense?"

"Because you're you." And yes…I appreciated the fact that most of the time he made logical sense.

Cooper popped up grinning, ignoring the frustration in Sawyer's voice and appreciating the game. "And why do you love me?"

That was easy—because he was Cooper. That wouldn't be good enough, though, even if it was true. "Because you're funny, and you see the best in people, and you're happy and loving."

Cooper gave Sawyer a side glance and stuck his tongue out. "See, that's better than not being nuts."

Laughing, I pinned both of them down to my chest. "Nope, not going to argue. Kiss and make up."

They both relaxed and leaned in to give each other a kiss. Deciding that they needed a surprise and something to get their minds off the conversation—which had gotten stressful in a way I hadn't expected—I took a second to frantically chase down an interesting idea.

"How about we go get pancakes for breakfast? It's actually breakfast, so Sawyer can try them this time." Cooper bounced up like he was one of those little rubber balls that slammed all over the room as soon as they got going. Sawyer gave me a knowing look as he sat up and nodded.

"That sounds good. Those chocolate chip ones Cooper was talking about sound fabulous." Sawyer leaned down and gave me a kiss, whispering a low "Thank you" in my ear. "Should we get ready to go right now? I'm starving."

The restaurant was open early, so I knew by the time we got dressed and ready, they'd have been open for quite a while. "That sounds perfect. I'm thinking strawberries and chocolate, personally."

Cooper was bouncing all over the bed, his naked dick swinging around like a dirty circus ride. He was listing all of the options he thought would be perfect, and from the sound of it, he would make himself sick if left there unsupervised.

Sawyer gave him an indulgent smile and climbed off the bed. "Okay, I'm getting a shower. I'm not sure he needs caffeine and sugar, though. I'm thinking eggs and toast for him."

Dodging a horrified Cooper, Sawyer laughed and hurried to the bathroom. As soon as the door was shut, Cooper threw himself into my arms. "Thank you for distracting him. It's what he needs."

Doing my best not to smile, I nodded. Yes, because of course, I'd just been distracting the other nut. "You're welcome, pup. How about you go use the guest room shower so we can hurry?"

He gave me a flirty look. "Who are you going to shower with?"

Resisting the urge to wrestle him down to the bed, I shook my head. "Neither. You're both going to wait to come until later. Now go get a shower before I forget I was planning on letting you orgasm today."

Cooper had that look like he was thinking about testing my resolve, but he nodded and scurried off the bed. He'd taken that entirely too easily. I knew that expression. "You're going to behave, aren't you, pup?"

He smiled innocently as he dashed out the door. "Of course, Master."

Yep. Entirely too easy.

13

COOPER

I COULDN'T DECIDE if I'd pushed him too far or not...but I'd ended up in my cock cage. Considering how erotic and just plain sexy it was, I still wasn't sure. That was probably the point. Since I'd tried to drive him crazy, he was just returning the favor.

I wiggled a little in the seat. If I could have convinced him to plug me too I could have—

"Cooper, stop that." Jackson's firm voice distracted me enough that I dropped my fork to my plate.

"What?" Picking up my fork, I looked around the table.

Sawyer snickered. Leaning close, he whispered, "You look like you just discovered what your cock is and won't leave it alone. Sit still before we get kicked out of here."

Sighing, I shook my head and whispered back, "I'm in the cage and can't get hard. You're nuts."

Jackson was staring across the table at us, trying not to laugh. He wasn't doing a very good job of it. Sawyer didn't see my logic. "Well, whatever you were doing, trying to get yourself off, stop."

He gestured to his pancakes. "I haven't even eaten half my

breakfast. If you get us kicked out before I finish, I'll never let you forget it."

He clearly hadn't consumed enough caffeine yet.

Before I could explain that to him, Jackson's fork appeared in front of my mouth with a huge bite of his pancakes. "Oh, thank you."

They were just as good as mine.

It had taken quite a bit of skill to talk him into the pancakes I wanted, but it had been worth it. He was enjoying them too, so I didn't feel guilty. The white chocolate and strawberry pancakes were almost sinfully delicious. But my dark chocolate and salted caramel ones with those little slices of almonds were incredible too.

I was going to have to order both of them again another time to compare them. It might take several trials before I had a clear winner. "I can't decide which ones I like better."

Jackson stole a bite of my pancakes, nodding in agreement. "I think you're right. It's a difficult choice."

"Hey, stop stealing my pancakes."

"I distinctly remember you telling me that we were going to share. I'm not sure you understand what that word means."

"You're not supposed to threaten to take away my pancakes." He should have known how sharing worked.

"Yes, we're going to have to work on that concept with you." It shouldn't have sounded dirty, but somehow as Jackson spoke, it sounded sexy and hot.

Reaching out across the booth, I speared another mouthful of pancakes. "And just how would you go about teaching me?"

Sawyer started to laugh but unfortunately, he'd been midswallow, so it turned into a coughing fit. Jackson and I both watched as he finally caught his breath and took a sip of his water. When he could breathe, I leaned in close, giving him a hug. "Are you okay?"

Sawyer nodded. "Yes, but you guys can't do that at the table. Or at least warn me."

"Warn you about what?" It wasn't like we'd been naked at the table.

"The dirty teasing and ridiculous innuendos." Jackson tried to give me a serious look, but he was still trying not to laugh, so he ruined it. "You know exactly what you did."

Maybe. "But I'm curious. There are so many interesting things he could mean."

"But we're not going to talk about them at breakfast." Sawyer didn't seem to be willing to budge on that.

I looked over at Jackson, hoping he'd intervene. "But—"

He shook his head before I could get the words out. "I'm going to have to agree with Sawyer on this one, pup. Between the wiggling and the teasing, you're going to get us in trouble. Don't you want to be able to come back here again?"

Sighing dramatically, I went back to focusing on my food. "Such drama queens. You're both being silly."

Sawyer leaned in close again, dropping his voice low. "We'd be silly if we both weren't already hard."

Interesting. "Is it because I'm locked up?"

Jackson shook his head. "Nope, pancakes or I'm going to finish them."

They were no fun at all. "All right."

I went back to focusing on my food, determined to keep my pancakes safe by eating them. Sawyer and Jackson ate slower, joking and laughing. I finally tuned back in when they started going over the plans for the day.

Jackson looked like a kid with a secret and had an excited tone in his voice. "No, I know exactly what we should do."

They'd been talking about errands and new movies that were out, but it looked like he had something else in mind. Sawyer gave him an amused look. "Is it a surprise, or are you going to tell us?"

Jackson was more excited than I'd ever seen him. It was like Christmas morning, and he was standing in front of the tree full of presents. "Cooper needs an office."

That wasn't quite enough information.

Sawyer nodded and made a *more* gesture with his hand as he chewed. Jackson finally started sharing the idea he'd clearly been thinking about for quite a while. "We talked about taking one of the guest rooms and turning it into an office for him."

He looked at us like he wanted to make sure we were on the same page and I nodded. Once he knew we were following, he continued. "I think that's what we should do this weekend. Classes begin next week, and I want to have everything ready. We need to figure out which room to use and how the layout needs to work. If it should be just an office or if there should be a bed in there too. That kind of thing."

We'd talked about it, but I kind of thought it was just one of those *what if* types of discussions. "You want to get it ready this weekend?"

He nodded enthusiastically. "Yes, it won't be that big of a project unless you want to paint. Then that might take us a few days, but if you like the colors, then all we have to do is go shopping and move around some furniture."

There was a part of me that winced at how expensive it would be to buy the furniture. But I had to remind myself that the money wouldn't be that big of a deal, and it was something he honestly wanted. The idea of having that much space just for me was daunting, though.

My gaze ping-ponged back and forth between them, and I nodded slowly. "You'll help me pick it out, right? I want it to look like it belongs with the rest of the house."

Jackson nodded understandingly. "Of course, but I want you to remember it's your office. So it needs to be something that you like too."

Sawyer leaned in close and nudged my shoulder with his.

"How about some shelves and a nice wide table? I'm sure we can find some fabulous options. It's stuff you'll be using for years, and sooner or later, you'll need a space for doing work at home."

He glanced over at Jackson and then back at me. "Eventually, we're going to have to get something organized for him too, because we're going to have to make him start using a desk and not the kitchen table."

I nodded, half-teasing, half-serious. "I think there's room in the house, or with a little bit of remodeling, there's space in the work building for a nicer office. That little one out there will work for Lee or whoever helps out, but he needs something more professional."

Sawyer nodded. "See, it makes sense for both of you. But yours first because you need it sooner. He's already been making do for a while, but we want you to start off on the right foot. And I think having your own space will keep you more focused. Less distractions that way."

He had a point. But as I turned to Jackson, he spoke. "That's a good idea. I'm going to need some time to figure out what will work best for me. This will give us practice setting up an office, so I'll be able to see what might work later."

"I guess so. Yes, that makes sense." I rolled the idea around in my head. "But I don't want to take too long before we find something for you."

"Of course, but one project at a time." Jackson pointed to my half-empty plate. "Hurry up and eat your breakfast, so we can go look at furniture stores."

"And maybe an office supply store for one of those big calendars?" It was starting to take shape in my mind, and I realized there were quite a few things that I needed to get.

Sawyer spoke up. "We probably need more pens and paper around the house. Maybe some notebooks for you? I think the only office supplies Jackson has are actually down in the office."

Smiling, I nodded. "Yes, I had to search through half the house the other day to find a pen."

"I think we have a good plan." Jackson was smiling like he'd solved the problem of world peace. I liked seeing him excited.

"Perfect." I was going to get an office.

MY OFFICE WAS TRYING TO KILL ME. THROWING MYSELF down on the guest room bed that we pushed into the corner, I groaned. "Why didn't we buy the shelf that was already built? Whose idea was this crazy mess?"

Sawyer leaned over me, trying not to look frustrated. "Yours, genius. Remember? You didn't want to spend the extra money for the ones in the shop that were already built."

"Somebody tell me when I'm being ridiculous. I clearly should not have been in charge of that decision." It hadn't looked like that many pieces in the store. Somehow they were multiplying like rabbits.

Before I could start to complain again, Jackson took Sawyer's place leaning over me. "How about we take a break?"

"Yes! We've been doing this for days."

Sawyer snorted. "It's been thirty minutes. And you're right. Next time I'm overruling you."

He was silent for a moment before he spoke again, this time with teasing laughter in his voice. "You know, all we have to do is talk to Jackson's dad and tell him that we need a lesson in how to put it together. I'm pretty sure he'd do it for us."

Jackson groaned. "You're not going to do that to me." He reached out and grabbed my hands, pulling me to my feet.

"We'll do something fun for a while and then come back to it later."

"What should we do?"

I couldn't decide if I was bored or tired or frustrated, but doing something else sounded wonderful. Maybe if finding the right furniture hadn't taken so long, this part would've been easier. But it had taken *forever* to find the perfect pieces. In my defense, however, they'd said it was my desk and that it should be exactly what I'd wanted.

They shouldn't say something they didn't mean.

Eventually, I'd found just the right desk and shelves, and we'd actually managed to get home before lunch. So it really wasn't that bad.

Jackson smiled. "How about I get everything out and you show me your sexy pup for a while?"

Oh, fabulous. "Yes!"

That was much better than following endless directions. I looked at Sawyer who was standing there shaking his head and smiling. "Come play with me too."

Sawyer's expression said he thought that sounded exhausting. "I'll throw the ball for you and watch you play, but I'm going to flop down on the couch and be lazy."

Deciding he was a lost cause, I turned to Jackson and smiled. "If I'm a good pup, do I get the cage off?"

He leaned down and gave me a kiss. "Possibly." Then his gaze heated, and I knew he was picturing all the fun things he could do to me. "But you look so sexy in your cage while you're playing."

I groaned. Partly in frustration, but partly because my dick found that idea fabulous and was trying to get hard. Its little brain made it impossible for him to remember that he was stuck. "But if I'm very good, you'll think about it?"

Leaning closer and giving him a teasing look didn't seem to be helping. His heated gaze seemed to intensify, but I wasn't making much progress on getting the cage off. "Oh, I'll think about it every moment that your sexy naked body runs around the room."

We seemed to have two different definitions of what it meant for him to think about changing his mind. But I wasn't going to push him at that point. I figured I had a pretty good chance that he'd let me come once he saw me needy and sexy. "Yes, Master."

Yep, the wicked look on his face said that he had devious things on his mind. My chances of coming seemed to be rapidly dwindling, but my chances of getting so turned on that I spontaneously combusted were going up dramatically.

I loved Master.

Pulling us close, he kissed both of our foreheads. "Sawyer, will you get him ready? I want to move things around in the living room."

"And lock the doors." We were still only at about fifty percent with that if I didn't remember to do it. Jackson was getting better—he didn't want anyone to walk in on us, but it wasn't something he'd ever had to focus on before.

His smile went from wicked to filled with humor. "And make sure the curtains are closed."

"Thank you." Stretching up, I gave him a kiss.

"Okay, you go get ready, and I'll fix everything else." He released his hold on us, and we got teasing smacks to our asses as we moved away.

Grabbing Sawyer's hand, I dragged him through the house to the bedroom. I didn't want to take any chances that they'd change their minds and insist we keep working on getting the office together. I wanted it all done, and I was getting excited, but that thing had more pieces than an Ikea kitchen.

Sawyer laughed as he followed me to the bedroom. "You're certainly excited."

"What do you think he's going to get out?" As soon as we entered the bedroom, I started stripping off clothes.

"You'll have to see." Sawyer's answer was too vague, but he'd begun helping me get naked, so I wasn't going to complain.

As my clothes came off, it got harder and harder to stay still. There was one less layer that kept Cooper in the front of my mind, and Maverick was coming to the surface. My pup had a name!

I'd been a little worried I'd end up a Rover or something crazy. Not that I thought Jackson would do a bad job—but naming something was hard. Pups had different personalities and needs. For Sawyer and me, a lot of our personalities showed through even stronger as pups, but I hadn't been sure how Jackson would see it.

Worrying had clearly been ridiculous. He'd done a fabulous job.

Once I was naked, Sawyer pointed to the middle of the floor. "Go wait for me."

The cock cage swung as I went over and got down on the floor. Once I was on my hands and knees, the cage felt even better. The weight was more pronounced, and it kept it right in the front of my mind.

Maverick was going to love running around with the tail rubbing so incredibly and the restraint keeping him from getting hard. The images in my head were enough to make my cock attempt to swell, and I moaned. It was going to be a sexy, insane, need-filled afternoon if Master didn't let me come.

I couldn't wait.

14

SAWYER

WATCHING him was exhausting and arousing at the same time. He bounded over the jumps and around the obstacle course Jackson had made for him. By the time he was halfway done with his third circuit, I was stretched out on the couch, trying not to yawn.

Jackson was watching and smiling as Maverick went through the course at full speed. Jackson's eyes seemed to be drawn to the cock cage that hung between Maverick's legs. When he'd first started walking around the living room and exploring all the toys as a pup, the little moans and distracted wiggles had both our gazes glued to his beautiful body.

He loved the way the restraint made him feel trapped and owned, and with the plug nudging his prostate every time he wagged his tail, it was even better. Jackson smiled and gave words of encouragement as Maverick played. My muscles ached as I watched, but none more so than my dick. He was a beautiful mix of happiness and desire.

Jackson sat down on the carpet as a panting Maverick came over to him, clearly begging to be petted. He gave Jackson a bark and wagged his tail fast enough for a low whimper to escape. Jackson chuckled and reached out to run his hands over Maverick's back. "I have a horny pup."

Jackson slid one hand down to Maverick's belly, where he pinched his nipples. The other hand moved lower down his back to rub his ass and nudge his tail. Maverick was in heaven. He wagged his tail and arched up, begging for more, but his frustrated little sounds let both of us know exactly what he really wanted.

Not that Jackson seemed to be in any hurry to give it to him.

No, Jackson was in full master mode and seemed perfectly content to tease and torment Maverick. Which probably pleased the naughty pup as much as being able to come. Jackson's hands kept up the light caresses until Maverick sounded almost frantic, and the tail was going so fast I thought he might come, even though he was restrained.

"Good pup." Jackson reached beside him and brought a glass of water with a straw in it to Maverick's mouth. When the pup was finished drinking, Jackson pulled it away and gave him another pat. "All right, go do it again." Jackson pointed to the course that wound its way through the living room and gave Maverick's haunches a pat.

Maverick whined and gave Jackson a pleading look that had Jackson shaking his head and issuing the order again. Maverick barked and turned to run through the course. The exercise kept him distracted enough that he'd have a harder time coming, but the movement of the cage and the pressure of the plug kept him on edge.

I hadn't completely understood at first how he could find the role as freeing and erotic as he did. As he'd talked about it and shared that part of himself with me, I'd gradually come to understand it. But my pup had never been like Cooper's, and that was fine with me. I liked the way it felt to let everything go.

Jackson kept him going until Maverick was completely lost

in his role and in the need that was building. As Maverick slowed, Jackson called him back over, waving a ball that he now had in his hands.

Maverick skidded to a halt in front of him, his chest heaving with exertion and his hips making little thrusts against the air. Jackson ran his hands gently over Maverick's back, soothing him but not willing to let the desires fade. Because as Maverick relaxed, Jackson's hands moved down to his tail to tease the sensitive skin.

Jackson reached down to cup even lower as he threw the toy across the room. I could only guess that he'd been teasing Maverick's balls from the breathless whine that came out of the pup as he shivered before chasing the toy that was rolling through the room.

They played ball for several long minutes and every time he brought it back, Jackson let his hands caress over his pup and kept the need pushing through him. The next time he rolled the ball and told Maverick to fetch, Jackson stood.

"I'll be right back, Maverick." Then he paused and looked at me. "Will you throw the ball for a few minutes? I want to grab some things from the bedroom."

Jackson's eyes sparkled, and I knew whatever he was getting would drive Maverick crazy. "Sure."

I forced myself to sit up and move down to the floor so Maverick could bring me the ball. I heard Jackson walk back to the bedroom, but I was focused on Maverick. With Jackson, he'd been trying to behave because all he wanted was to come. With me, teasing was the only thing on his mind.

He'd move close and shake his head, pretending to let me grab the ball. Before I could get it, though, he'd jump back just out of reach. His head and chest would go down to the floor and his haunches would arch up with his tail going at a furious rate.

He thought he was so funny.

It took so long to get the ball from him, I only had time to throw it once before Jackson came back. His hands were hidden behind his back, and Maverick and I both stilled to watch him. Jackson grinned ear to ear as he came to sit beside me.

I heard something behind his back as he set whatever it was on the floor, but I couldn't picture what made the sounds. It was probably some kind of toy for Maverick, but nothing that we had came to mind.

"Come here, Maverick." Jackson brought one hand around to the front. His fist was wrapped around something, but I still wasn't sure what made the odd, almost rattling noise. Maverick barked and moved to Jackson. His body was wiggling, and excitement radiated from him as he watched Jackson's hand.

I grinned and Maverick gave a frustrated bark as Jackson opened his hand, showing the leather cock ring that would wrap around Maverick's erection. He'd be able to get hard, but orgasming wouldn't be any easier. The only thing that would be easier was Jackson's ability to make him even crazier.

"Roll over, boy." Jackson's firm order had Maverick rolling over obediently, the tail still going madly as he stared at his master's hand.

Jackson ran his fingers over Maverick's belly and down toward his trapped cock, but took his time before moving to actually take off the cage. The whoosh of Maverick's tail on the floor and the whimpers that escaped had me so hard, I found myself frustrated as the desire to play with my own cock mounted.

When Jackson finally took off the cage, we both sighed in relief, but it was short-lived for Maverick. It took a handful of strokes to get him so erect, I thought he'd come right then. Before he could slide over the edge to the pleasure he desperately wanted, Jackson quickly had the other restraint wrapped around Maverick's erection.

Maverick's hips jerked up, and he gave a low bark, but when Jackson wrapped his hand around the aching flesh, Maverick whimpered and made needy sounds that had Jackson reaching down to adjust his own dick.

"You look so beautiful, Maverick." Jackson's slow caresses and tender words only made us both more turned on. Just watching him touch Maverick made my dick jerk. "Are you ready for your surprise, pup?"

Jackson didn't wait for a response. "Roll over, Maverick. Good boy. Sit."

As Maverick obeyed the instructions, Jackson reached behind him again. Pulling out an odd-looking ball, he held it so Maverick could see it. "I have a surprise."

Smiling, he waited a few moments before explaining what it was to me. "This is meant to have a treat inside it, but I put a smaller ball in here. If he manages to get the small ball out, then he's going to get to come. But he can only use his mouth."

Jackson turned his head back to focus on Maverick. "No paws, Maverick."

Maverick watched the ball intently, his cock jerking as he focused on it. Jackson squeezed it with his hand, and the ball opened at several seams. They would have been big enough for a dog treat to fall out if it was turned the right way, but Maverick's mouth wasn't that big, so it would be a lot more difficult.

Jackson was clearly pleased with his find and ran a hand down Maverick's belly to give his cock several slow strokes. Maverick whimpered again. His body seemed to vibrate with need, but he kept his eye on the ball.

Finally releasing Maverick's erection, Jackson threw the toy to the other side of the room where it ricocheted like there was something alive inside it. The little ball in the middle seemed to give it an extra bounce it might not normally have had. Maverick bounded off with a bark as he scrambled around the room, chasing the insane ball. His cock bounced and jerked, probably making him crazy, but he looked excited as he barked and ran after it.

Jackson chuckled and moved to pull me closer as we watched. When I was nestled between his legs, he leaned back against the couch. Resting against his chest, I wasn't sure if I was going to be able to relax or not. The feel of his body wrapped around mine and the way his erection pressed against my back was making it almost impossible.

When he absently ran one hand up and down my chest as he watched, I started to think that letting me relax wasn't on his agenda. When both hands came up to slowly caress around my nipples, I *knew* he had other plans.

As turned on and frustrated as Maverick was, I wasn't sure how much teasing he had in mind for me. Fingers plucked and pinched at my nubs, making me groan. With every noise that escaped out of my mouth, Maverick lost focus on the ball and looked over at me distractedly.

"Don't you want to come, Maverick?" The words were for his pup, but he pinched my nipples, making me arch up and cry out. Maverick went back to madly trying to figure out how to get the ball out, but I knew he wasn't as focused as he tried to pretend.

When Jackson's hands moved down my chest, I couldn't decide if I was relieved or not. I wasn't sure what he was planning as his hands skimmed gently over my chest, but when he pulled up my shirt, I wasn't surprised. "Let's get this off you."

I sat up so he could strip it off me, but before I could lean back, he was pulling me against his chest again. I was stretched out and felt a bit like I was on display for him. I thought he'd go back to playing with my nipples, but instead, his hands moved to my pants.

I groaned as he worked the zipper down over my sensitive

erection. He chuckled and stayed focused on freeing my cock. When he had my pants open, he shoved my underwear down under my balls. That made everything stand out more prominently and made me feel wicked in an erotic way.

I was displayed and available for my master to use, however he saw fit.

Cooper was definitely rubbing off on me.

I hoped that he'd keep going, but he went back to teasing my nipples and slowly caressing my erection. Making me come didn't seem to be his goal. Master absently teased at my body while he watched Maverick play.

Maverick was shaking it with his mouth, trying to figure out a way to get the little toy out when Master pinched my nipple again and squeezed down on my dick. I cried out in pleasure, and it was enough to startle Maverick into dropping the ball.

It immediately rolled away, so he had to start chasing it again. But his body didn't really want to cooperate. His hips kept jerking, trying to grind his cock against anything that would give it pleasure, and he kept turning to watch me squirm and moan.

Every time he got close to grabbing it, Jackson would pinch something or tease me, so I would cry out again. It was driving us both to the edge. Maverick finally managed to catch the ball, and Master went back to slowly teasing me.

"I think I'll let you come once he gets the ball out, Sawyer." Master's words were low, but they slammed into us. We both moaned in frustration, but it seemed to give Maverick a renewed passion in getting the damned little ball out.

Master continued to stroke and caress me, but it was never enough to make me come. Every time I got close, he'd change the way he touched me. I couldn't decide if he knew me that well or if it was just intuitive, but whatever it was, all I could do was moan and make little pleading noises.

"You're both doing so good. Look, Sawyer, Maverick almost

has it." Master rubbed slow circles over the sensitive head of my dick as we both watched Maverick desperately working at the toy.

His head had the ball pressed down on the floor, and he was frantically trying to get the openings wide enough to get the ball out without losing control of it completely. I tried to stay quiet, but it was just too much, and I finally cried out, pleading to come.

Maverick jerked, and the ball popped out from under his head, flying across the room as the pressure was released. Master chuckled and slowly jerked me off again. "Oh, he almost had it."

Master was absolutely wicked.

When Maverick had the ball again, Master tightened his grip, pushing me toward my orgasm. I tried to hold back and fight the pleasure, but it was too much. The sounds ripped out of me as I got closer, but that time, Maverick managed to ignore it.

I wasn't sure if he was that desperate or if he'd sunk so far into his puppy persona that nothing else mattered but the toy and the reward. It was probably a mix of both. But I didn't care. I just wanted to come.

When the tiny ball fell onto the carpet, we were both stunned. Maverick quickly started barking and frantically ran to us, his hard cock bouncing and dripping precum.

"That's a good pup." Master praised Maverick as his grip tightened on my cock, and he pinched one nipple. "Didn't he do a good job, Sawyer?"

Fuck, he wanted me to talk?

"Yes, Master." The words were low and I heard the desire dripping from them, but I managed to get them out. I wasn't going to do anything that gave him a reason to take my orgasm away.

"You've both done such a good job. What did I say would

happen when he got the toy out of the ball?" Master's voice was filled with a wicked pleasure, and I knew he loved drawing out the final moments.

Maverick whimpered, and I saw another drop of precum hit the floor. We were both so close. "That we would get to come… when he got the ball…we could come."

"That's right." His hand moved faster over my dick. "Come for me, Sawyer. Show Maverick how good it's going to be when he gets to come."

I wasn't sure if it was the order or the way he finally gave me enough to push me over, but cum exploded out of my cock as my orgasm barreled over me. Master's hand kept jerking me off and teasing my nipples to keep the pleasure going, and all I could do was lie there and let him have me. It was incredible.

Finally, it was all too much, and the pleasure began to fade. When I squirmed, Master released my cock and one hand stroked my chest slowly. I closed my eyes and relaxed into his touch.

"Roll over." The firm order was followed by frantic movement as Maverick obeyed, presenting his belly and hard dick.

I heard Maverick whine, and I pictured Master releasing his cock. "Wag, Maverick."

The tail had to be going a thousand miles an hour as he whimpered and barked. When he finally let out a low, pleasured sound, I knew he was close. I could feel Master's arm start to move faster.

"Come." The quiet order had me opening my eyes, and I saw Maverick's orgasm slam through him. He shook, and his hips thrust up to push his cock even harder into Master's hand. It didn't surprise me that it hadn't taken much to make him orgasm. He'd been ready since he'd first started running around the room, and watching me come had only made the need worse.

When he was spent as well and lying limply on the carpet, Jackson carefully eased the tail out of him and set it aside. Cooper rolled over and put his head on Jackson's leg before he flopped back down, exhausted by the small movement.

Smiling, Jackson ran his hand tenderly over Cooper's head. "We need to make time for this more often. Especially times where you both get to play and run around. We're going to sit down soon and actually put it on the calendar."

Cooper nodded sleepily and yawned, making me fight off a matching one. Planning it out was a good idea, but it would have to wait until I had more energy. Cooper seemed to agree.

Jackson shifted to take off his mitts and knee pads, but when he moved to the collar, Cooper stopped him. "Not yet, Master. I like having it on."

I knew what he meant. The weight felt safe and secure around his neck. It made him feel loved and owned in a very basic way that the words didn't quite hit. He knew Jackson loved him, but when the collar was around his neck, the love had a tangible feel that sank deep into him.

"That's just fine, baby." Jackson's hands went back to stroking us slowly, and I closed my eyes. I could almost feel the press of the collar. The floor wasn't comfortable, and I knew I was probably squishing Jackson, but it was perfect, and I never wanted to move.

15

JACKSON

WEARING them out had taken more time than I'd expected, but they napped long enough for me to get the office finished. Without Cooper's scattered attempts to put the shelf together and Sawyer's impatience with Cooper's unorganized enthusiasm, it actually went quickly.

Cooper had been right, however. It'd come in a thousand pieces.

Luckily, the desk was more streamlined and had to have been designed by a separate team, because it had a much more logical construction. If drunk monkeys designed the shelf, the desk had been designed well enough that a drunk monkey could put it together.

By the time the boys stumbled out of the bedroom, I had the guest-room-slash-office finished. Eventually, the plan was to get the bed out completely and make it a full office. For the time being, they both worked fairly well together. The only thing that hadn't really fit was the dresser. But it hadn't taken me long to realize that it would work in our bedroom. As long as we did a little bit of furniture shuffling.

Not wanting to wake them up, I, moved the dresser out into

the hall. With the room completed, I realized how bare it was. We'd taken long enough looking for the actual furniture that we hadn't picked up any of the office supplies Cooper needed.

Cooper's head popped around the corner, and his sleepy expression changed quickly to a beaming smile. "Oh, it looks perfect."

I gave a little shrug and nodded. "I think it turned out pretty well. You picked out some nice pieces."

I'd have bought him anything he wanted, but he'd picked out some inexpensive but nice-looking furniture. Depending on what career path he took, I figured we could change out the furniture gradually. But for the time being, they would work perfectly, and he hadn't cringed at the price.

We'd been working on discussing financial decisions together, but they were still getting used to the fact that as a family, our income was bigger than they'd expected. With all three of us working, there was a lot of discretionary income.

Eventually, I wanted to get them set up with more long-term savings, but getting them settled in the house and making it feel like a home for them was my first priority. They were young enough; we didn't have to worry about their retirement savings right away.

As he walked into the room, I went over and gave him a quick kiss. "You have to be starving, but once we eat, I thought we could go back out and pick up the office supplies now that we have a place to put them."

I wasn't sure how he would feel about the idea. I knew if I'd suggested it earlier, he would have found a reason to complain. But as he looked around the room, I realized that between getting to come and playing, he'd calmed down and had gotten a good second wind. He nodded slowly and looked at everything with a more critical eye.

"Yeah, that's probably a good idea." He turned and gave me a hug. "Thank you for getting it all put together."

"You're welcome." I gave him another kiss and smiled as his stomach rumbled. "Should we go look for food?"

He nodded. "Sawyer is already digging around in the kitchen, so he might have found something. Hopefully, it will be enough to share."

"Agreed. I think there's plenty of leftovers, though. Oh, and we should probably lay out something for dinner, so we don't forget." As we headed out of the office, Cooper looked at the dresser. "Where is this going to go?"

"I thought about taking it to the bedroom, so you guys have more space." We'd had to get creative, fitting three people's clothing into one room, and too much of their stuff was still in all kinds of odd places.

"That's a good idea. But let's worry about that later. Food first." He took my hand and started enthusiastically hurrying me to the kitchen.

Laughing, I nodded. "Yes, that will wait until later. First is food, then office supplies, and then we'll figure the rest out."

Sawyer closed the refrigerator as we walked into the kitchen. "What about later?"

His arms were loaded down with containers, and it looked like he'd had the same thought I did. When he went back to the refrigerator, I realized we probably needed to clean it out. I'd lost track of whose responsibility it was, but that probably didn't matter. The whole idea of chores and the division of labor needed to be reevaluated.

"We thought about going to the office supply store after lunch." I glanced over at the clock on the stove and shrugged. "Well, after our late lunch."

Sawyer nodded. "Yeah, if we're still going over to your parents' house tomorrow, that's probably the best idea."

Cooper bypassed the food and went immediately over to the coffeepot. Bouncing around the kitchen excitedly, he had new coffee made and a large mug doctored up before I figured out what I wanted for lunch.

When he started heading over to the table without looking at the food, I put my foot down. "Oh no, go find something to eat. We're not going to the store when all you've had is caffeine and sugar."

He set the mug down and blinked up at me sweetly. "Yes, Master."

Shaking my head, I walked over and pulled him into my arms. "Cheeky boy. Do I need to get the cock cage out again?"

He had to think about that entirely too long before he shook his head. "I'll be good."

Not believing him for a minute, I pointed to the counter. "Food. If we wait too much longer, we'll never get anything done."

He couldn't argue with that. "Yeah, we'll end up watching a movie or cuddling, and the day will get away from us."

"And I want everything ready for you by Monday. You're going to do a great job, but that means having all the right tools." Having a separate space so we didn't distract him would be a big part of that. I knew firsthand how difficult it was to sit in the living room and do paperwork when they were goofing off in the bedroom or watching TV. It wasn't the noise, but being able to see that they were having fun while I had to work. I wanted to make studying as easy as I could for him.

Sawyer grabbed his plate from the microwave and turned around. "Was there anything else we needed to do?"

I shrugged. "Nothing that I can think of."

There were always errands to run and things to do, but there was nothing that stuck out in my head. "Let's head over to the office store in the big shopping center. That way if there's something else we were supposed to do, it might jog your memory."

"Oh, they have one of those big warehouse clubs over there. Wouldn't that be fun—"

Sawyer started shaking his head before he reached the table. "Nope. Going to the grocery store takes long enough. There's absolutely no reason to torture us like that."

I wouldn't have phrased it exactly that way, but I had to agree with Sawyer. Cooper would have entirely too much fun bouncing around between free samples and loading up the cart with all kinds of things we didn't need. "I'm not sure the kitchen has the storage space for that kind of store."

Wanting to get things back on track, I went over to the counter. I glanced down at the food and gave Cooper a pointed look. "I'm going to have some of the stir-fry from the other night. What about you?"

Cooper gave a dramatic sigh but walked over to look through the containers. It didn't take long for him to make a decision, and soon we were back at the table with Sawyer. As I watched them eat, I thought back to how my life had been just a few months before. I would've never imagined sitting around the table with my two loving partners, but they were perfect.

"COOPER, IF YOU DON'T PUT THAT DOWN, THEY'RE GOING TO kick us out of here." He should not have been able to find that many phallic objects in the office supply aisle at Target.

He giggled and put the oddly shaped stapler down. "Come on, they make it too easy."

"That's not the point." Sawyer pushed the cart closer to Cooper and tried to get him back on track. "You said you wanted options that were more fun. That's why we came here. Next time, I'm going to tell you no."

Trying not to smile, I turned to Cooper. "I'm just going to ask better questions. Because I think we were had."

I wasn't sure if he was having too much fun looking at all the office supplies or if he was beginning to get overwhelmed. We'd picked up a few things at the office warehouse store, but some of the stuff there had been a little bit too businesslike.

There hadn't been enough things that screamed out Cooper to me, so I'd understood where he was coming from. But the trip had rapidly devolved from finding office supplies to finding dirty things to drive Sawyer crazy with.

Cooper grinned but went back to picking out the supplies he liked with more efficiency. After a few minutes of gathering notebooks with intricate designs on the front and pens in a variety of colors, he moved down and looked at the whiteboards.

We'd looked at several at the other store, but he hadn't found anything that he loved. I'd wanted the space to feel like his, so if it took us multiple stores, that was fine with me. It was probably the first space he'd ever had that was just his. His parents had seemed controlling enough, even in that one quick instance, that there was a pretty good chance he hadn't been able to decorate his room growing up.

As often as he said he wanted it to feel like the rest of the house, I knew he was trying to think of us. But even in a house that we shared, there still needed to be space just for them. Watching Sawyer look around at the different office supplies reminded me that he needed his own spot as well.

I wasn't sure he needed an office, but he should have a space that was just his, even if it was small.

After a few more minutes of debating over whiteboards for his office and picking up another package of pens, as well as a cup to put them in that said Brats Do It Better, we seemed to be done. Sawyer gave a dramatic sigh of relief as we walked away.

As he started for the front of the store, Sawyer stopped the cart. "Oh, I remember what we were supposed to do. Your mother said she was going to go buy hamburgers and asked us to bring dessert."

"Yes, thank you for remembering." There were too many options.

"What do you guys want to do?" I pointed back over to the small food section, trying to think it through.

"We can grab a box of brownie mix or something like that if you want." I reached into my pocket and pulled out my phone. "I'm not sure if the bakery is still open. We might be able to catch them, but I don't know what kind of selection they'll have this late."

Cooper shrugged. "Brownies sound good...or maybe cookies."

Sawyer nodded, not seeming to care. "Either one sounds fine. I don't think we need to go rushing to the bakery, though."

"Okay, let's head over and see what they have." Sawyer turned the cart around as we started heading back toward the grocery area of the store. "Brownies or cookies? If you want cookies, I think we have everything to make some at home. But we'd need to grab chocolate chips or something like that to go in them."

Cooper seemed to think about it. "Cookies sound good, but brownies would be quicker, right?"

"Yes, with the brownies, we can mix it up and pop it in the oven but with the cookies, forming them and baking them is a little bit of a longer process unless we buy the already made refrigerated ones."

Nodding, he smiled. "Then let's do the brownies. I want to get the office set up later and hopefully, have time to watch a movie or something tonight."

"I like that idea. We'll make cookies another day." I had a feeling Cooper would love getting his hands messy in the dough.

His smile turned into a teasing grin. "But maybe we should

get two boxes, just to make sure we have enough for everybody and that they turn out right, of course."

Pretending to take the request seriously, I nodded like he'd said something wise. "Yes, brownies can be so temperamental. You never know how many the box will make."

Sawyer barked out a laugh and shook his head, rolling his eyes. "You're such an enabler. He doesn't need two boxes of brownies."

But before they could start that debate, we heard a familiar voice that had everyone quieting down. Melissa was talking with someone a few aisles over, and at first, I thought she had to be on the phone. It wasn't until I heard a male voice responding to her that I realized she was there with someone.

Sawyer's eyes widened, and Cooper giggled quietly. They'd been curious about Melissa's new man, but things had been so busy I hadn't been able to bug her. Cooper had texted her several times, but she'd been very cagey with the details.

As their voices got closer, I couldn't decide what we should do. It'd been clear that she wasn't ready to introduce him to the family yet. Deciding to abide by her wishes, at least for the time being, I gestured to the next aisle.

Cooper gave us a wicked grin but followed us quietly. Part of me agreed with Cooper, teasing her would've been fun. But without knowing the specifics of their relationship, it wouldn't have been fair to her. We caught a quick glance of him as they walked past our aisle, oblivious to their audience.

They were talking intently, but Melissa seemed relaxed and happy with him. They looked like any traditional couple. Nothing about their relationship seemed unique or interesting, but glancing at my own family, I knew that appearances didn't always tell you what was under the surface.

When they were far enough away that they wouldn't hear us, Cooper finally laughed. "He's cute. I mean, he looks like some kind of banker or something."

Sawyer grinned. "He should be out playing golf or something."

"Driving her crazy tomorrow is perfectly acceptable, right?" I glanced between the two laughing faces. "We gave her privacy today, so it's only fair that we get back at her tomorrow." They immediately nodded.

Even Sawyer couldn't argue with the logic. "She showed up at your house knowing we were there. I think we behaved admirably today."

Cooper nodded earnestly. "And if she's stingy on the details, I'll invite her for lunch next week. She'll say yes on the off chance she can be nosy about us."

Laughing, we headed back to get the brownie mix. I ran my hand over Cooper's head and gave his shoulder a squeeze. "She'll never know what hit her."

His innocent little shrug and wide-eyed expression had Sawyer and me in stitches. Oh yes, he'd have the entire story of their relationship before lunch arrived. She'd never seen my little secret weapon at his most devious.

I WAS REALLY GOING to have to remember to go to bed earlier on Saturday nights. That or drink more coffee on Sunday mornings. But the idea of missing out on sexy or even just cuddly times with Jackson and Sawyer was too sad to contemplate. I'd catch up on sleep later in the week. It was starting to become part of my routine lately.

"More coffee it is." Leaning my head back against the wall, I fought off a yawn.

"To be honest, I'm not sure you need more coffee." April's teasing voice coming from the door made me jump.

I laughed once I caught my breath. "Don't do that."

"See? And that proves my point."

"Bullshit. That just means I need to put a bell on you or something, like a cat." Sitting up, I shifted my legs out of the way, so she could sit down in the other chair. "Has it finally quieted down?"

"Not really, but my taking a break now was a better option than honestly answering the woman who always asks why we don't have the fun pink drinks too. I can't handle her today." April sighed and slouched back in the chair.

"Yeah, she's been a bit obsessed lately. We always play the 'What's new that I'll like?' game, but every time it ends with her ordering the same black coffee. Last week, I offered to put red food coloring in a white chocolate mocha if she wanted something pink I could put whipped cream on. She said black coffee was fine."

"You didn't?"

"Of course I did. And she can't complain, because I was trying to give her something she'd like." I wasn't going to feel bad about teasing that old bat. At first, we'd all been nice to her. We'd thought she was old and had dementia or something, but it hadn't taken long to realize she just liked being a pain in the ass.

My new goal in life was to get old enough that I could do whatever I wanted, and people still had to be nice to me.

"I don't understand some people." April was too nice sometimes. "I still think something might be wrong."

And just not devious enough.

"Uh, no. I talked to the guy at the barbecue place down the street the other day when he was out back on a smoke break."

Her face drew up in a wince. "Oh gross, but he's so hot."

"I know. Wrinkles by the time he's thirty, but what can you do?" Not to mention cancer and everything else. "Don't distract me. What was I saying?"

Maybe I had imbibed a bit too much caffeine.

"Smoking guy and pink coffee lady."

"Oh, yes, she goes in there every Friday and tries to convince them to make her a hamburger. They get a long song and dance about the company motto of putting customers first and their wood-fired ovens making a better burger before she just orders macaroni-and-cheese."

"You're kidding." April started to laugh but still looked like she felt guilty.

"Nope. Evidently, she pulls that crap all over town because

she's bored." That was a direct quote from another customer who'd gleefully tattled on the old bat once she was out of earshot. But I wasn't going to repeat who'd told me. They were not-so-friendly neighbors, and she'd made me promise.

Shaking her head, the last of her guilt seemed to fade away. "Some people are nuts."

"Or need a hobby."

"You know, we'll have to be even more careful since she's not sick. She's probably the type to leave a crazy review."

"Aren't you the person who told me that I can't please everyone after that asshole left a review on Yelp about me?" Some people really didn't like being told no.

She rolled her eyes. "He got upset when you wouldn't sell him a hot dog. That's not the same thing."

"He was high as a kite but somehow still managed to find Yelp on his phone." The things people could do without thinking these days still surprised me.

She giggled. "That's still the best review ever though, and at least he didn't mention you by name."

"No, he called me 'that twink Bob who refused to sell him a wiener.' I'm not sure that's any better." I couldn't have made that shit up. I sounded like some kind of hooker until it became clearer that he'd been talking about a hot dog.

Laughing, and looking much more relaxed than she had when she'd sat down, April sat up like she'd just gotten a genius idea. "I forgot."

"That's not enough information."

She frowned at me. "I wasn't done."

"Then don't pause in the middle." *Duh.*

"The other building fell through. They thought everything was a done deal, but at the last minute, there was a problem with the old owner. A lien on the property that he hadn't disclosed. They have to start all over, finding a new location." She grinned like it was one of Willy Wonka's Golden Tickets.

"Why's that good?"

"Because it gives you more time to get going on the college stuff before they begin looking for managers."

"Oh." Yeah, more caffeine. That had taken entirely too long to grasp. "How long do you think it will set them back?"

"A few months at least. That will give you enough time to show them you're serious and not just talking about it."

"Do you think that will make a difference?"

She shrugged. "I'd think so. If I was looking to hire, that would be something I'd think about. Someone who might be all talk versus someone who's actively working toward a goal is a big deal."

Was it bad that I was glad the deal had fallen through? Probably.

Was I going to *feel* bad about it? Nope.

I was going to show them that I was the best candidate for manager ever.

"It's perfect." Okay, so it was slightly lopsided and leaned toward the left for some reason, but it was sturdy and would be perfect for a little bird family. "Look."

Sawyer was finishing up the last nail and didn't immediately follow directions. Once his was done, he looked over, giving me a goofy smile. "It's fabulous."

"I know." I turned it around, so he could see the rest of my perfection. "It's going to look great once it's painted."

"That part's going to have to wait. I think the food's almost done, and if we make them wait while we paint, they're not going to be fit to live with. Jackson's a lot like his mom, but don't let that polite exterior fool you. He'll get revenge if he needs to." Jackson's dad laughed. "You should hear more of the stories from when he and Melissa were kids. They spent more time grounded than not until they learned to get a little bit better at finding good ways to get back at each other."

Daniel was hilarious.

He'd spent the entire time we'd been in the garage telling us stories from when Jackson was little. I couldn't imagine my parents ever telling funny stories like he did, and from the look on Sawyer's face, neither could he.

His childhood hadn't exactly been the most loving. Every time we came over and spent time with Jackson's parents, it was like he was seeing the kind of family he should have had. Sometimes he was quiet as we drove home, but for the most part, it didn't make him sad. I thought he was happy that not everyone's parents sucked or found it difficult to accept when they were wrong.

I loved the fact that Master had a wonderful family.

He wouldn't have turned out to be the perfect man for us without them. It really was sad that there were no Hallmark cards for that kind of thing. *Thank you for raising my master to be a wonderful and loving person. Happy Father's Day.*

Yup, the greeting card industry needed more diversity.

"Dinner's almost ready. No more playing with those birdhouses." Jackson's mother's voice had us smiling. It was like she had radar for when we even thought about her.

"Told you, boys." He turned toward the garage door and called out to her. "We'll be right there, Charlie."

He listened for a moment for a response, but when she didn't call out any other instructions, he turned back to us. "All right, let's get it cleaned up so we can eat." Daniel pointed to the shelf on the other side of the garage. "Why don't you go put the scraps over there?"

As we cleaned up, I saw him poke at my birdhouse when he thought my back was to him. He was intently analyzing my amazing feat of engineering. Sawyer saw him marveling and laughed. "It's like the Leaning Tower of Pisa."

"Because it's fabulous and it's going to be iconic." It was unique and incredible. My first project was going to amaze Jackson.

Sawyer smirked, making Daniel laugh. "Sure, we'll go with that."

He was just jealous that his looked so traditional. Who wanted that when you could have memorable and interesting? "Jackson's going to love it."

Daniel nodded and seemed to be relieved not to have to debate how fabulous my birdhouse was with Sawyer. "It's going to look good in the yard when you're done. Have you picked out a spot for it yet? You might need to get Jackson to put a post by the back of the house for it. That way it won't be too far from the window."

"That's a great idea. Oh, I'll get a bird feeder to go with it." That way I'd be guaranteed to get more birds.

"Don't go buying that. We can make it after you finish with the birdhouse. I'm still researching everything for the dollhouse, so we've got time." He gestured toward the long table in the back filled with papers and odd bits of wood.

I wasn't sure what research entailed, but he seemed to be doing a very thorough job. "I think it's going to turn out great. Are you sure we can help?"

He nodded, but even I couldn't miss the sideways glance he gave my birdhouse. I smiled. "My projects are very sturdy."

That was one of the most important things for the birds. They had to feel secure in their home. The fact that it would be beautiful too was going to be a bonus. Daniel smiled and seemed to love being able to agree with me. He was so cute. "Absolutely. You're going to make a very sturdy dollhouse."

"You boys put everything away. Daniel, you stop distracting them." Charlotte's voice called out louder that time, and Daniel groaned.

"We'll be right there."

"That's what you said a few minutes ago. We're not going off *retirement time*, Daniel Kent."

Daniel rolled his eyes. "That woman needs a hobby."

They were so funny it was impossible to keep a straight face; even Sawyer couldn't do it. Trying to hide our smiles, we finished cleaning everything up and headed out of the garage. Daniel kept puttering around, mostly talking to himself.

I thought he was doing it just to drive her nuts.

Jackson was sitting at the picnic table at the back of the yard, talking with Melissa and grinning. He'd obviously wasted no time in teasing her about hanging out with her new man at Target. When they'd moved to the "Let's run errands together" phase, it was clear they were serious.

Leaning close to Sawyer, I whispered, "What do you think she's saying?"

"What is that daughter of mine up to now?" Charlotte's voice came from behind us, making me jump.

Sawyer tripped over his own feet and barely managed to catch himself. I looked at her with a perfectly confused expression. "What do you mean?"

She gave me a skeptical look, and I could tell she was studying me. When I didn't give anything away, she cocked her head and gave me a small smile. "Never mind. Are you two ready to eat? I've been trying to get Jackson and Melissa to come grab food for a few minutes already, but they seem to be very distracted."

I was really going to have to work with Jackson on his subtlety.

I shrugged and gave her another confused look while Sawyer tried not to look guilty. "Maybe it's a sibling thing. I'm an only child."

I hadn't meant to bring up a sore subject, but she frowned and looked kind of sad. Shoot, had something happened to one of her siblings? People's families could be such a minefield.

Before I could figure out what to say, she stepped forward and wrapped one arm around me. "Come talk with me for a moment. Sawyer, why don't you go tell those two *not-so-secret agents* it's time for dinner."

He nodded slowly but gave me a worried look as he walked off. Mothers like Charlotte Kent were not something we had any practice in dealing with. I wasn't sure if we could've said no, much less if we should have.

Once we were alone, she walked me over toward the patio furniture near the back of the house. "How are you doing, Cooper?"

That was a very loaded question. "I'm fine."

But was she?

Charlotte still had that emotional look I couldn't quite define. "I heard you saw your parents in the store the other day."

Oh.

I wasn't sure what to say. Was she upset by them showing up too? I'd never really thought about the fact that when Jackson became part of our family, his parents had become part of ours too. "Are you okay? Jackson got kind of upset over them."

I didn't think that was oversharing. She was his mother. She had to have realized he was a worrier when it came to things like that.

Charlotte cocked her head again and looked at me like I was a curious piece of art. Sawyer and I had gone to a museum one time because they were having a day where you didn't have to pay to see the paintings. He'd had that expression several times during that trip.

"I'm okay. I'm just worried about you. Did you talk to Jackson about it?"

"Yes, I thought maybe not mentioning it would be easier for him, but he's a talk it out kind of guy. Once we discussed it, he was more relaxed." He and Sawyer both had been more at ease the past couple of days.

She smiled and nodded, reminding me a lot of Jackson. He looked so much like his dad that it always surprised me when she did something that I could see in him. "I'm glad. I want you to know that you can come talk to me if you ever need anything. I know that you have Jackson and Sawyer, but sometimes you might need another person to talk to."

Worriers were kind of exhausting, but it always made me feel better when they were happy again. "Thank you. I'll remember that."

Not that I was going to do something that might upset her again.

"Why don't you help me chase everyone down? Sawyer seems to have gotten sucked into whatever my two children are cooking up back there. You go tell them if they don't get over here right now, I'm going to expect a three-page report by the end of the week." She was serious; I could see that. But when I stood there staring at her, confused, she waved her hands in a shooing motion.

"Yes, ma'am."

Mothers were so odd sometimes.

Hurrying across the yard, I tried to figure out what she'd meant, but there wasn't enough to go on. When I got to the picnic table, I gave all of them dirty looks as they smiled in greeting. "Jackson, your mother says if you don't get over there right now you'll both have to write a paper by the end of the week? I have no idea what that means, but it's got to be a punishment of some kind, and I haven't done anything wrong."

I was starting to think that he'd gotten his Dom side from his mother.

Weird.

I wasn't going to be punished when I'd been good, though.

They both mumbled low curse words under their breaths

and stood up. Sawyer was grinning, but Jackson shook his head. "She's going to drive me crazy."

That was basically what his mother had said, so I thought it was kind of cute.

"What does she mean?"

Jackson wrapped an arm around me and took Sawyer's hand as we crossed the yard. "She used to make us write papers about what we'd done wrong. She said it was to help us realize how to make better choices."

Melissa snorted. "It was just to see if our stories matched up and try to catch who was at fault."

"Well, obviously you two never learned, because she knows something is up." They both needed lessons in how not to look guilty.

Sawyer laughed and nodded. "That's what I said."

I was surrounded by amateurs. "And I bet you two haven't even gotten your story straight yet?"

They both at least had the good sense to look guilty as they nodded. "Oh, for goodness' sake."

They clearly needed a keeper. I hoped the story was good enough for all the crazy we were going to have to deal with. "I'll get you out of this, but my birdhouse is going to get its own special stand, and I want it to be right outside the back door, so everyone can see how perfectly incredible it is."

He was going to owe me, and I was going to collect in sex and birdhouses.

17

SAWYER

"HOW IS MY LITTLE ENERGIZER BUNNY?" Jackson spoke quietly as I walked into the living room.

"Finally asleep."

Flopping down on the couch, I curled up next to Jackson. I sighed as I rested my head on his shoulder. "One minute he was awake and going ninety miles an hour about bird feeders, birthdays, and blowjobs, and the next minute he was out. Don't be surprised if you wake up with your cock in his mouth. He went to bed horny and you know what—"

Jackson stiffened and interrupted what I was saying. "Hold on. The blowjob part makes sense. And he fell asleep in the car on the way home from my parents' house. He needed sleep, not sex, but what was he saying about birthdays?"

"I completely agree with you about the sex. He was exhausted. But um...the birthday thing was actually something I should have mentioned sooner. His birthday is Friday." The surprise on his face made me feel bad, and I winced. "Sorry, it slipped my mind. I should've said something about it before, but in the past, our budget for celebrations was so small, all we did was get more expensive takeout and watch a movie at home."

Jackson nodded, but I could see conflict and a variety of emotions running across his face. Excitement, frustration, and worry seemed to be at odds. "Did he say what he wanted to do this year? Does he want to keep the same traditions you guys have established or do something else?"

"You're overthinking this." I curled back into him and rested my head on his chest. Sitting on the couch, it wasn't the most comfortable position, but it would work. "You're talking about Cooper. What do you think he said?"

Jackson seemed to relax, and then a low chuckle escaped. "Knowing him, he probably started going on about Disney World or something like that. Hopefully, he dialed it back to something reasonable, because I don't think any of us could take a vacation at this short notice."

He was so cute.

There was nothing about the fact that it would be expensive, or just ridiculous; his first thought was that we couldn't take time off. "Very close. He was actually talking about Universal Studios. He's seen one too many commercials about Harry Potter World lately."

I could hear the smile in Jackson's voice again, and his whole body shook with laughter. "Of course, how could I have guessed wrong? What did he finally settle on? We're going to have to wait until he's at a semester break in his classes before we do something like that."

Smiling, I nodded. There were other vacations he probably wanted to go on more than standing in line with a bunch of tourists for a bank-themed roller coaster. If he wanted to plan something like that, though, I wasn't going to stop him. "We talked about going out to dinner to someplace nice. Other than that, not much."

Cooper was a go big or go home kind of guy, so when he couldn't go big, all he could think of was curling up on the couch with us and being the one to pick out the movie.

"Okay, I'll talk to him this week and see what sounds good, and then I'll make reservations somewhere. Does he want the whole family there or just us?"

That had me stumped. I knew what the question meant, but it hadn't occurred to me that anyone else might want to come. "Will your family want to come?"

Jackson didn't have to think before he responded. "Of course. We usually go out to a nice restaurant. The birthday person gets a few presents, and then we either have dessert at the restaurant or go to my parents' house and have dessert there, depending on what they want. Birthday individual's choice and all that, you know."

"But we're not exactly...I mean, the three of us are family, but I hadn't really thought about how your parents or sister would see it." They'd all accepted us really well, so I probably should have expected it.

"Melissa is going to see it as an excuse for more presents. My parents understand how important you guys are to me, and I think they're starting to see you as part of the family. They haven't said anything specific, but the way they treat you and ask about you guys makes it feel like they're adopting you into the family as just more kids."

"Kinky, but I appreciate it. Cooper's fantasies might run off the rails into weird on that one, though, so you might want to keep that comparison to yourself. Or find a less taboo way to describe it." Laughter rolled through Jackson's body as a chuckle escaped.

"Okay, I'll find another way to explain that. But yeah, Cooper would have a field day with it." The way Jackson said it made it sound like he would be willing to humor Cooper no matter what the fantasy involved.

Those two and their dirty role-playing fantasies.

That one would be a bit much for me, however. "Let's save that one for a night when I have to work late. Deal?"

"I don't know what you're talking about." The laughter in his voice made the lie completely unbelievable. I sat up enough to look at his face, and his eyes were sparkling.

"Your performance, to make that lie believable, would need to be Cooper quality. So don't even try. Just nod and say, 'Yes, Sawyer.'"

Quiet laughter rolled through the living room. "Yes, Sawyer."

"Thank you."

Jackson's arms wrapped tighter around me, and I moved back so I was curled into his chest again. I loved the way his words seemed to rumble out of his chest when my ear was pressed against it. "You don't mind that, right?"

It wasn't a real sentence, but I thought I knew what he'd meant.

"That you guys will play and do different things when I'm not around? No, it's fine. Cooper's imagination always goes lightning fast and is so detailed. I like the fact that he has somebody to do it with. I tried and did my best in the past, but it's not quite the same without someone who enjoys it as much as he does."

I loved the fact that between us both, we could give Cooper what he needed. From stability to dirty fun, there wasn't anything he was missing. I didn't have to worry I wasn't giving him everything he needed, or that it wasn't quite enough. He was happy and surrounded by love, and that was everything I'd ever wanted for him.

The fact that Jackson was everything I needed as well was a bonus.

He was strong and stable when I needed it, and sweet and fun when it was time to relax. If I picked out every quality that I thought our master should have had and designed him myself, I couldn't have made a better master for us.

Jackson's hands caressed along my back, and he shifted

sideways on the couch, so he could pull me onto his lap. When we were both comfortably settled, and I was curled up on his chest as we stretched out on the couch, his hands started the soothing motion again.

"He's so much fun to play with, but I want to make sure we're not doing anything that frustrates or upsets you. I also don't want you to feel left out. It's important we all have strong relationships with each other and not just as the three of us, but—"

I tried not to smile, but it was hard. He was so sweet. "No, it's fine. Honest. It's not something I'm drawn to, so I like that you guys can play around like that together. What we do already is enough for me."

The puppy play and the domination were everything I needed. I could understand why things like the role-playing were fun for them and why Cooper got so turned on pretending to be Jackson's wicked virgin, but it wasn't something that got me going.

"I like our time together too. Baking with you and going out to dinner was a lot of fun." I felt Jackson kiss the top of my head, and I lifted it up just enough to let him know I wanted another one. His lips touched mine, and his arms tightened around me to deepen the kiss. We sucked and teased each other until we were breathless.

When I finally pulled back and rested against his chest again, I was hard and Cooper's birthday was the last thing on my mind. We'd plan that later. We had the evening to ourselves, and I wanted to make the most of it.

Grinding my cock slowly against his thigh, I let my fingers caress his chest. I wasn't as brazen as Cooper, but I knew how to get my point across. Jackson's hands rubbed my back again, but they began massaging harder and working their way lower. When they reached my ass, he continued the rough kneading, which just pushed my erection harder against him.

The slow build of pleasure continued until I moaned and pushed my ass up, silently begging for more. Jackson's grip tightened, and he pulled me roughly up his chest. Lifting my face, I offered my lips up again as he squeezed my ass and continued the sexy rocking motion.

The need continued to build as he made love to my mouth, fucking it with his tongue like I knew he wanted to do to my ass. Like we both wanted him to do to my ass. Whimpering into his mouth, I wrapped my arms around his neck and rocked my hips back, trying to show him how much I needed him.

When Jackson finally released me, he kissed down my neck and whispered, "Do you want more? I can feel how hard you are. Is that what you want? Do you want to come, love?"

"Yes...but not just that...I want you to make love to me." I didn't just want to come. I didn't just want his hand or lips wrapped around my dick. I wanted everything. I needed to feel him inside of me.

"Whatever you want, my sweet boy." Jackson's words sent a flood of emotion through me, but it was the way his teeth nipped at the juncture of my neck and shoulder that made me moan again.

He gave a low chuckle and licked the sensitive skin before nibbling on it again. "I'll kiss you and lick you and taste you and get you all ready for me. Then I'm going to slide deep inside you. Is that what you want?"

God, yes. "Please...yes..." His damned teeth and wandering hands were making it hard to think.

He laughed low and wicked, letting me know he understood exactly how crazy he was making me, before letting his tongue lick up my neck again. Jackson's hands moved off my ass, but instead of caressing up my back again, he roughly shoved them down the back of my jeans.

The pants were just loose enough that they fit, but it made the front tighten and suddenly my dick was pressed against the zipper, making me gasp and precum shoot out. His sexy, low laugh sent sparks through me as he nibbled on my ear and squeezed my butt.

He hadn't touched my hole, but the way he kneaded and separated my cheeks made me feel open and empty. The rough teasing had me moaning and writhing against him. I hadn't even gotten naked, and between the feel of his hands and the way my cock was trapped and felt almost bound, it was nearly too much.

My whimpers grew more frantic as his fingers slowly worked their way toward my clenched opening without ever going all the way. He was the master of teasing and drawing out pleasure.

Jackson seemed to love edging more than anything else, and his passion for it showed. The fact that Cooper and I both loved to be teased and Cooper loved denial so much made us the perfect fit for our sexy master.

"Please...please...I need...Master..." The desperate words spilled out of me before I thought about what I would say.

Jackson's answer to my pleas was to let his fingers ghost over my entrance and to bite down on my ear, making me shake and buck in his arms. I was going to come if he kept it up. "Please. I want you to be inside me when I come. Please."

"My sweet boy...then that's what I'm going to give you. But you know I'm going to take my time, don't you?" He shouldn't be able to make words sound wicked and tender at the same time, but somehow he did.

"Yes, just, please...I need more, Master." Sometimes he was just Jackson when we made love, but when he started taking control and letting me know my orgasm would be on his schedule alone, he became Master in my head again.

"Good boy." His tongue flicked out to lick the area where he'd just nibbled, and it made me moan. The way he was thrusting my cock against his body had me shaking and whimpering. He was in control and it was incredible.

When his hands relaxed, I wasn't sure what to expect. As he pulled them out of my pants, my moan was in frustration and disappointment. Jackson chuckled again and gave my ass a pat that had a flash of needy embarrassment running through me.

"Lie down on the floor, Sawyer. I want to be able to stretch out and kiss you much more thoroughly than I can on the couch." The quiet words were almost growled out. I knew part of it was so that we didn't wake Cooper—he really had been exhausted—but I could hear the desire thick in his voice.

"Yes, Master." Climbing off him was harder than it should have been. My legs didn't want to work, and my dick was so hard it made everything else uncoordinated. Finally, I managed to make it off the couch and on to the floor without falling or looking stupid.

No, the way Jackson's eyes watched me, and the heated way his gaze followed every movement said he loved just how turned on he'd made me. Before I could lie down, he was there beside me. "Let's get this off you."

He quickly stripped me of my shirt, and the heat from his hands as he started exploring had another shiver racing through me. "My pants too...please..."

Any embarrassment I might have felt in the past about begging faded away. All I wanted was to have my dick free and his touch *everywhere*. I'd do whatever it took to get them both. He always kept his word, though, so I didn't think I'd have to wait much longer. He'd promised to take his time, and that generally meant naked, so he could tease over every inch of me.

Relief flooded through me when he laughed but reached for the button on my jeans. As he stripped me out of them, I arched into his touch, any subtlety falling away as I grew more desperate. When he had the jeans and underwear to my knees, he moved closer and his hands caressed around my hips to grab my ass again. "I bet that feels better, doesn't it?"

"Yes, thank you." Okay, part of me could see why Cooper loved role-playing so much. It was easy to picture the fantasy of promising Master anything he wanted because he'd let my dick free. The reality of his touch as his hands slowly slid over my ass was even better, though.

"I want to give you everything you need. Don't I? It's just going to be at my pace." The sexy but frustrating words made me moan.

He was such a tease.

"Yes, Master."

He tugged me close until my cock was pressed against his still-clothed body and leaned down to kiss me. I loved being with him any way he wanted, but when it was like this...tender but commanding, while I was naked and he was dressed, it was perfect. It made my submission swell inside of me and everything just fell away.

Master took his time kissing me and teasing me like he'd done on the couch, but eventually, he was ready for more. My cock was painfully erect as he slowly rocked my hips, humping me against his thigh. When he pulled away, I whimpered and my dick jerked like it was trying to reach out to him for more.

Ignoring my protest, Master laid me down on the carpet and finished stripping off my pants, so I was completely naked for him. "So beautiful."

Master kissed down my body, alternating between delicate licks and stinging bites. It wasn't hard enough to mark my skin, but I could feel his teeth as he moved away. The incredible sensation as he nibbled along my body was like little lightning bolts shooting straight down to my dick.

When his slow exploration of my chest finally reached my hip, and he worked his way toward my cock, I almost couldn't breathe. The idea of those nibbling little bites around my cock or down my shaft had precum leaking out of it.

I wasn't sure if I was relieved or disappointed when it was the slow licks that teased at my erection. Every little sting of his teeth would have been magnified, but the fantasy wouldn't leave my head. When Master finally took my shaft between his lips, I groaned in pleasure, and his hands pinning my hips to the floor were the only thing that kept me from thrusting up into him.

He lightly sucked on the head, making me gasp and shake before letting it slide deep into his mouth. All I could do was moan and alternate between basking in the pleasure and begging for more. When his hands moved from my hips down to my thighs and spread my legs apart, I knew what would happen next.

Master stretched out between my legs and opened me up, so he could continue kissing and exploring as thoroughly as he'd said he would. When he kissed down my balls and licking them all I could do was squirm, but when his tongue finally reached my hole, even begging was too hard.

"That's my beautiful Sawyer. Show me just how much you want it. Let me hear those sexy noises." His tongue licked around my clenched muscles, and all I wanted was more. Every touch made me greedier, and all I could think about was feeling him inside me and finally getting to come.

Dirty sounds of pleasure and pleading noises flooded out of me as he kept sending me higher. When his tongue stiffened, and he fucked me with it, all I managed was a whimper. As his mouth moved away and a finger took its place, I finally found the words to beg for what I'd wanted for so long.

"Please. Make love to me, Master. Fuck me, please. I can't wait. I'm going to come. Please." My balls were snug to my body, and everything felt tight and heavy like I was right on the verge of coming, but I wanted him inside me when it finally happened.

Jackson gave my hole a kiss before stretching up over me. "If you come before I give you permission, you'll have to be punished." One hand braced his body over me and the other came down to start tweaking and pinching my nipples. "Is that what you need?"

My brain couldn't work enough to find the right answer. I'd take any punishment as long as he let me come and as long as he slid his cock deep inside of me. "I'll be good. Please." I lifted my head and gave him a kiss. "Make love to me, Master. I want to be good for you."

A shiver ran through Jackson, and he moaned against my lips. "If that's what my boy wants."

When he sat up and kneeled between my legs, all I could do was hold my breath. When he reached into the side table drawer and grabbed the lube, I moaned.

No condoms. Just lube.

Feeling him inside me and feeling his cum mark me was something I thought I'd never get used to. When he tossed the lube beside my hip and started reaching for his clothes, everything inside of me sighed in anticipation.

It was finally time.

Lying stretched out on the floor, I watched him slowly take his clothes off. I wanted to reach up and strip him down as fast as I could, but that wasn't what he wanted. No, he wanted to make me wait and to let the need build.

When he was finally naked, he moved back between my legs and reached for the lube. It seemed to take forever until his slicked fingers were reaching for my hole. It was all too much. I clamped my eyes closed as his fingers teased around the tight ring of muscle. As one finger finally slid in, I moaned and fought to relax my body.

I wanted to feel him inside me as fast as possible.

The teasing finally stopped when I got desperately close to the edge. One finger moved to two and when I was begging for more as the third finger eased into me he finally said I was ready.

Thank fuck was my first thought, but I was smart enough to keep that to myself. Master's dirty laughter echoed through the room again, letting me know I hadn't been as careful as I'd thought. As his fingers came out of me, I opened my eyes and stared up into his face.

He was stretched out over me again with his cock positioned at my ass and his arms bracing my legs. Leaning down, he took my lips in a long, heated kiss as his cock pressed against my body. I moaned into Jackson's mouth as his dick sank deep into me. Lifting my hips, I fucked myself on his cock.

It was Jackson's turn to moan as my tight body clenched around him, pulling him deeper. All thoughts of going slowly seemed to have left his mind when he saw how eager I was. He pulled back and fucked me in long, hard strokes.

I'd been on the edge too long to wait. I wanted to feel him inside me forever, but I was going to come no matter how much I wanted to stretch it out. With every thrust, my cock rubbed between our bodies, and I could feel my orgasm start to rush forward.

"Please." The words were almost impossible as I frantically tried to get them out. "I'm going to...please...come..."

His wicked grin said how much he loved the broken words. He'd pushed every thought out of my head, and all that was left was need and love. That was enough for Jackson, though. He shifted my legs and fucked me harder, the head of his cock brushing over my prostate with every pass.

"Now." When he finally slammed his cock into my sensitive bundle of nerves and ground his stomach against my dick, I exploded.

Cum shot out of me as wave after wave of pleasure went through me. My orgasm pushed him over the edge as well. I felt

Jackson's body shake above me and he finally lost his steady rhythm as he flooded me with his cum.

Marking me.

Claiming me.

Loving me.

When the pleasure had faded for both of us, Jackson eased his cock out of me and rolled us over, so he could wrap himself around me. He peppered my face with kisses as he held me tight. "Love you. My sweet boy."

I was done. All I could do was murmur low words of love back and curl into him. Every time we made love, it was like the first time all over again.

Passionate and loving and perfect.

18

JACKSON

"OKAY, SO THAT DIDN'T WORK." Staring at the phone, I frowned and found myself drumming my fingers on the desk. The dinged-up wooden top and metal legs were definitely starting to show their wear. When I'd first gotten it, I'd just appreciated that it'd been nearly free. But Cooper was right; I really did need a better office now.

Refusing to get sidetracked, I looked back down at the computer screen and tried to figure out another search term. Finding someone who made leather collars for *people* should not have been that difficult.

If I wanted cheap knockoffs of a movie, there were any number of adult novelty items I could find in the area. But there was nothing like what I was looking for. I'd found similar things on websites that ranged from megastores to small crafting websites that looked like they were run out of their house. None of which were very good options. I didn't want leather collars made in China, and I didn't want to give my credit card information to a kinky housewife that could have been halfway around the world.

"There has to be somebody local who does this." At least *reasonably* local. We couldn't be the only people within a couple of hours' drive who were in an unconventional relationship.

I'd spent entirely too much of the morning looking up numbers for every adult-based enterprise in the area. Most of them hadn't opened until later in the day, however, so I'd been forced to obsess over it all morning.

I was starting to run out of time, though. I had classes in about thirty minutes, and the closest lead I'd had was that the guy who ran the adult video store downtown thought there was some kind of BDSM club about two hours away.

That meant there had to be a reasonable number of people in the lifestyle, but it didn't help me with the information I was looking for. My next step was going to be figuring out if clubs like that had websites that were informative.

Probably not.

I wasn't sure if calling would help. If the situations were reversed, I wasn't sure I'd give out personal information to someone who called over the phone. Yes, I was looking for a business. But people still wanted their privacy, and I had to assume there were enough assholes out there that they would be cautious.

The sound of the slamming car door reminded me of how late it was getting. The clomp of Lee's boots echoed through the building as she got closer. She stepped into the doorway, smiling. The quiet individual who'd first applied had eventually blossomed into a happy person who seemed eager to come to work. "How's it going, Boss?"

"Good. I think I have everything ready for the first class, but can you double-check? I've got a few things I need to finish up before everyone gets here, and I know I missed something." I'd been too distracted when I'd set it up. "I'll be out there in just a few minutes."

She nodded and glanced at the desk. "Anything I can help you with?"

I tried not to look awkward as I shook my head. "No, Cooper's birthday is at the end of the week, and I'm just ironing things out."

That was basically the truth, so it came out smoother than I'd expected. Lee nodded and headed out the door. "Good luck on that, but birthdays are hard."

Oh yes—especially when I was buying for two special occasions and not just one.

His actual birthday present had been easy to buy. It'd taken some convincing to talk Sawyer into it, but we'd ended up wrapping up all kinds of information about Universal Studios. He'd know right away what the paperwork meant.

Just for fun, I'd also ordered a T-shirt and some cute Harry Potter things to go in the box as well. Sawyer thought I'd gone overboard, but I was already trying to figure out what we would do for his birthday. Luckily, I had several months to plan and get ready.

He was going to be harder to shop for.

The remaining minutes before my class started went by too fast. Before I'd found another business to call, it was time to get ready. The next couple of hours flew by in a sea of dogs and owners. Lee was a huge help, but I had a hard time keeping my brain in the game.

Between classes, I went back to my desk and made notes about different places where I might be able to find information, but I hadn't been able to make any calls. Knowing I only had about thirty minutes before Cooper and Sawyer would be expecting me back at the house, I mentally rearranged the rest of my to-do list.

"Lee, can you see what you can do to clean up before you go? I'll come down early and finish the rest of it in the morning.

I have a few things I need to do now." I was supposed to be looking at schedules and seeing if I could find room for another advanced class, but that would have to wait—same with the billing and updating the website.

"Sure, that's fine. I don't have classes tomorrow morning. Do you want me to come down and help with the paperwork?" She gave me a look like she already knew the answer, but I hated throwing extra hours on her that she hadn't planned.

"Are you sure? I don't want to take all of your time for studying or just hanging out with friends." Lee wasn't really much of a joiner, but I didn't want to keep her from having a life outside of work.

She shook her head. "This is better than just sitting around playing video games and chatting online."

"If you're sure, I could use the help." Especially if I wanted to have everything caught up, so I'd have more time for my boys over the weekend.

"It's not a problem." She was straightforward enough that I knew she'd tell me if I was scheduling her for too many hours.

But it was still difficult to get used to having someone around who could help. I had a feeling she thought I was being stubborn, but sometimes I just didn't think about asking her to do more work. I was getting better about it, however.

"Great then, I need help with updating some of the accounting and the website primarily. You pick one and I'll do the other."

"You need a better billing system and an accountant." She shook her head and for a moment, it was easy to see Sawyer standing there giving me the same lecture.

"You're right. The guys have given me the same speech. I'm going to be looking for an accountant who can help me get everything set up soon." But that just added something else to my to-do list.

Lee gave me a look like she didn't believe me for a minute before shoving me off to the office. Cooper would have been proud. I actually remembered to close the door before I started down my list. Three calls later, I was no closer to finding someone who made collars. I had, however, found someone who made fantasy shaped dildos and two more adult stores that were even less help than the first one.

And really, how many stores that just sold porn and vibrators did one area need?

All of that was online now, so I wasn't sure how they were staying in business. Before I could start down that unfortunate mental path, there was a knock on the door. "Come in."

The door opened, and Lee stood there for a long moment, giving me a curious look. "Everything's all cleaned up, and I'll see you about nine tomorrow. That should still give us plenty of time before your afternoon classes to get everything updated and organized."

"Perfect. Thank you." I wasn't sure if it would take that much time, but it was probably better to schedule too much time than too little.

"You really have no poker face, Boss." She shook her head and handed me a piece of paper she'd pulled out of her pocket. "Here's the number for a local accountant who does a lot of small businesses. She looks really vanilla, but don't be surprised if something interesting comes out of her mouth."

Oh. "Um, thank you?"

I wasn't sure what else to say.

Lee snickered. "We both know you would've taken another six months before you found somebody. We're going to get all the books updated tomorrow and in a reasonable order, and you're going to call her and schedule an appointment." Lee looked at me like she was expecting an argument but wouldn't accept it.

"Perfect." The disbelief on her face was almost comical. "Don't look at me like I'm crazy. I'm not going to put it off for the hell of it. If she works out, that's great. It's taking up too much of my day." I'd heard the speech numerous times from Sawyer, and he was right. My time was better served teaching more classes or just having time for a hobby.

Lee looked pleased with herself and seemed to stand a little bit straighter. "All right. For the next thing on your to-do list…"

I couldn't remember telling her anything else on my to-do list.

The look on her face changed, and it reminded me of Cooper before he started complaining that we needed to lock the doors. "Closing the door to make personal phone calls is great and all, Boss. But if you really want to keep things private, then you can't leave weird to-do lists all over the desk and then send me in here to look for paperwork."

Shit.

"I apologize for that. It won't happen again."

Shit.

Shit.

Shit.

Lee didn't look as shocked or as horrified as I'd imagined, so I could only assume she wasn't offended. It still wasn't something that had been appropriate for the workplace, so I was lucky things hadn't turned out worse.

One eyebrow went up, and her expression said I was being ridiculous. "Do I look so vanilla that you think I wouldn't know what collars are?"

There was no good way to answer that question, so I fell back on my original apology. "It's still not professional for work, and I apologize."

I got an exasperated look, and she shook her head. "Give this guy a call."

She pulled out another slip of paper from her pocket and held it out. "He mostly does custom pieces, and his schedule is usually pretty full, but he said he can work in two collars this week. Next time you need something done, it's going to take more advanced notice. You need to plan better, Boss, and not wait until the last minute."

What. The. Hell.

I must have stared at her for too long. She snorted and shook her head again. "Just say, 'Thank you, Lee,' and give him a call now. I told him you have some ideas and stuff already planned out."

"Thank you, Lee." See? I could follow instructions.

"You're welcome, Boss." Her smirk peeked out again, and I knew she was silently laughing at me. "Have fun this weekend."

I alternated between embarrassment and pride. Pride won. "Thank you. I'm looking forward to it."

"It's not what I was expecting when I first started working here, but good for you." She glanced over at the clock on the wall. "Okay, I have to go." She paused for a moment and seemed to be making a decision. "I've got a date to get ready for."

Were we starting to share more personal things about our lives, or was it some kind of fair's-fair mentality? I wasn't sure. And what was the most appropriate answer?

Have fun?

No, that sounded too boring.

I'm glad you found someone?

No, that sounded like I thought she hadn't been dating enough or that she needed to date.

Fuck.

"What are you guys planning to do? Dinner or something more outside the box?" That sounded okay, right? Not too judgmental or too personal. It didn't ask specifics about her date she might not be ready to share and didn't assume gender or orientation. Cooper would tell me that I was overthinking it, but I didn't care.

Lee smiled and relaxed a bit more. "There's a coffee shop not far from campus that has live music some nights. We're going to hang out there for a while, and if we click, then dinner."

"Good plan. I've been stuck on long dinner dates with some incredibly boring people, and it's painful."

Laughing, she nodded sympathetically. "I bet dinners out are much more entertaining now."

"Oh yes. Especially with Cooper around." My lovable handful was an endless source of stories and fun.

Giving me a wave, she nodded and headed out. "See ya tomorrow, Boss. And don't worry, I won't say anything to anyone."

"Yes, and thank you." The idea that she might have said something honestly hadn't occurred to me. She wasn't the gossipy type.

"Welcome. Call him now so you don't forget."

I was getting instructions from my employee about calling a guy who made BDSM collars. Life took weird turns very quickly.

"No, you cannot wear a party hat to dinner." Sawyer's voice wasn't exactly angry, but I could hear his frustration mounting as I came into the kitchen. He turned and gave me an exasperated look. "This is all your fault. You have to fix it. I'm not going to dinner with him while he's wearing a party hat."

Okay, so it was my fault.

Cooper had been so excited as we'd walked past a display of balloons and party supplies in the grocery store that I hadn't been able to tell him no. Which was how we ended up with a living room full of balloons and a package of party hats that he insisted on wearing everywhere just to drive Sawyer crazy. I thought Cooper's goal was to fix it so he would have very thorough birthday spankings.

Trying not to smile, I turned and looked at Cooper. He was wandering excitedly around the room, giving longing glances to the refrigerator. "Cooper, no birthday cake. And what did we say about the hats?"

I got his best innocent look, and he sighed sweetly. "I'm sorry. I'm not supposed to wear it outside the house."

He took off the brightly colored hat and walked over to set it on the table. Then my wicked little nut gave Sawyer a big kiss and apologized. I didn't buy it for a second. I gave up trying not to smile but was still shaking my head.

Any time he looked that innocent, he'd done something naughty.

Walking over to my boys, I gave Cooper a long look and held out my hand. He tried to give me those big Bambi eyes, but I didn't budge. Finally, he sighed again, that time in frustration. "You guys are no fun. They wouldn't have minded. Your dad would have thought I was funny."

Cooper reached into his back pocket and pulled out another party hat.

"Thank you. Now, is that it?" I was learning to ask better questions.

He rolled his eyes but reached into his other back pocket. As he handed me the second hat, he deflated a little.

The little con-artist.

"Cooper, why don't we wear the hats out in public?" The conversation was starting to become too familiar.

"Because it makes Sawyer uncomfortable and that wouldn't be nice, and because they make me look too young. We'll all probably get arrested."

"And?"

"And if I really wanted to wear the hats, we should've had the party at Chuck E. Cheese's. I picked the nice restaurant, so we have to dress appropriately." Then the little imp threw himself into my arms and grinned. "But don't they look fabulous?"

"Yes, you always look incredible. But the lady in the grocery store asked us if you were having a big party for the kids in your class." She was older and seemed to be having trouble reading the labels on the groceries, so in all likelihood, she hadn't been able to see either of us very clearly, but it'd still made me nervous.

Cooper gave me a suggestive pout. "What? You don't want to be my sexy daddy?"

Before I could respond, Sawyer burst out laughing. "The look on his face says he wouldn't mind that at all. But for the love of God, don't say anything like that in front of his parents. Melissa will have a field day."

Cooper giggled, not promising to behave.

That was just to make Sawyer crazy, however. As excited as he was about his birthday dinner, I knew he liked my family too much to deliberately do anything that might embarrass them. We all knew eventually something would pop out accidentally. I was okay with that. We'd handle it no matter what it was, and I knew my parents wouldn't really care.

Aside from some interesting questions.

Giving him a quick kiss, I pulled away slightly and turned toward the refrigerator. "Now what did you do to the cheesecake?"

They both looked guilty.

I looked at Sawyer and shook my head. "You too? I thought he was the one I'd have to worry about. The deal was that we were supposed to leave it alone until tonight."

They both shrugged. "All right, let's see."

Heading over to the fridge, I opened the door and had to laugh. What had been a beautiful cheesecake with an absolutely perfect finish now had a good-sized slice missing from it. I looked over at my two guilty boys and raised one eyebrow.

Sawyer was the first to fess up.

"It was just a little piece. Well, a little piece for both of us." Then he neatly threw Cooper under the bus. "Cooper said he didn't think I'd made it right, and that we had to taste it before your family got here."

"Hey!"

Sawyer shrugged. "Well, you did."

It was Cooper's turn to throw him under the bus. "You said you didn't believe me for a second, and that I was just trying to manipulate you."

I couldn't believe it. They were the funniest people I'd ever met. "Hmm, I wonder what's worse...trying to manipulate someone into getting your way or letting someone manipulate you because you wanted to misbehave too?"

They both immediately pointed to the other like some kind of comedy routine. I was barely containing my laughter. "I had a special surprise for both of you tonight, but I'm starting to think —"

"What is it? Another birthday surprise?" Cooper's excitement was almost at a volcanic level.

"No, not a birthday surprise. Something else entirely." That had both of them giving me curious looks.

Cooper's eyes widened. "But —"

Sawyer's hand reached out and clamped over Cooper's mouth. He nodded and smiled just as innocently as Cooper would have if the situation had been reversed. "We'll be good."

Cooper gave Sawyer a dirty look once the hand moved away, but he nodded sweetly at me.

"I thought you'd say that." Shutting the fridge, I walked over and gave them both kisses. "Come on, you two. We're going to be late if we don't leave now. But don't think you're in the clear over the cheesecake. You're going to have to explain to my mother why there's a piece missing."

Their mouths dropped open, and they spoke in unison. "Shit."

19

COOPER

PRESENTS AND CHEESECAKE and steak and oh...the chocolate cake looked good.

"Cooper. What looks good to you?" Charlotte's voice pulled me back to what I was supposed to be doing—picking out dinner.

"Um..." Why couldn't she have waited another couple of minutes to ask me that question?

Sawyer laughed under his breath as I tried to figure out something to say. I hadn't actually made it past the dessert section of the menu yet.

Jackson leaned over to see what I was doing and smiled. "How about you try the other side of the menu?"

My chances of getting the chocolate cake were dwindling rapidly. "Good idea."

I didn't notice the waiter standing there quietly until Jackson's mother turned to address him. "We're going to need a few more minutes, thank you."

Oops.

It was the second time he'd come by. I thought he was just an eager beaver who couldn't wait for his tip, but I kept that to myself. I hadn't been looking at the menu for that long. I wasn't the only one still browsing the menu either. Daniel couldn't seem to decide what he wanted.

Turning the menu over so I could focus on the dinners instead of the desserts, it didn't take that long to figure out what I wanted. "Steak and shrimp."

Setting the menu down, I took a sip of water and looked around the table. Sawyer was sitting on one side of me and Jackson on the other. Jackson was grinning, but Sawyer sighed. "You couldn't have done that ten minutes ago?"

I shrugged. "I needed time to consider the decision. Then it was easy to make up my mind."

Neither one of them seemed to believe me, and even Melissa was trying not to giggle across the table. Jackson cleared his throat and leaned down to whisper. "That would have been more believable if we'd seen you look at anything but the dessert side of the menu."

I blinked up at him innocently and shrugged, not willing to admit defeat. They couldn't prove it. Deciding that a change of topic was a good idea, I looked across the table at Melissa and smiled. "How was your week?"

What I really wanted to ask her was how work had gone, or if she'd gotten everything ready for her new book that was set to come out soon. But we were all still pretending that no one knew about the books. Eventually, someone was going to have to take the first step in talking about the elephant in the room.

My goal was that it wouldn't be me.

I was going to keep my mouth shut. And I was really glad that with all her stuff going on, we weren't the most interesting people in the family. We actually seemed pretty normal and boring. I loved it. That made it much more likely that I wouldn't get in trouble.

Listening to the questions that Daniel could've come up with would have been funny, though. But I'd promised Jackson not to torture him. I'd gotten backed into a corner with that when Sawyer had agreed with Jackson and said he didn't want that conversation either.

Her reply was too cautious to seem natural. We were going to have to work on her subterfuge skills. "Not bad, busy."

Jackson was caught in a tough spot.

He desperately wanted to laugh and point out how obvious it was that she was hiding something. But he also didn't want the nature of our relationship to become public knowledge to the family, so he was trying to behave. It was incredibly difficult for him. Watching the two of them interact, it made me wish I had a sibling growing up.

But really, Sawyer probably filled that role—which was better because I got to have sex with him.

I wasn't sure what to say, so I smiled and nodded. "That's good."

Did that mean everything was all ready for the release? Did that mean she'd worked a ninety-hour week between both jobs and getting everything finalized? I liked hearing about her writing and how everything worked in general. It was a little bit frustrating having all the questions off-limits.

Sawyer stepped into the lull in the conversation and turned to Daniel. "How is the planning coming for the dollhouse?"

Charlotte couldn't seem to decide if she wanted to sigh or roll her eyes. She'd probably had enough of the dollhouse conversations, but Sawyer and I thought it was fabulous.

Daniel beamed. "It's coming along nicely. I started practicing making some of the different pieces this week and they're turning out very well."

"Wonderful. I can't wait to see how it will look." I wasn't sure if his description meant he'd just spent the week trying to make roofing shingles and some of the delicate cuts, but he seemed to be having fun, and that was all that mattered.

The small talk about everyone's week continued until the

waiter came back. He seemed relieved that we were finally ready to order. After a few minutes of getting everything organized and explained to the waiter, I thought I'd finally waited long enough. "When do I get to open presents?"

Laughter flowed around the table, and I smiled excitedly. Jackson reached out and ran a hand over my hair. "What, you don't want to wait until we get home?"

"Do I have to?" I made a show of glancing down at the long, flat box that was propped against his chair.

I was assuming that since everyone had brought their presents to dinner, it meant I didn't have to wait. At least, that was going to be my logic if they tried to pull a fast one. Waiting only made everything better with sex, not gifts or rewards.

Presents didn't work like orgasms. They didn't get bigger the longer you waited.

Jackson looked like he was going to tease me, but Charlotte spoke up, shaking her head. "No, it's your birthday. If you would like to open them now, that's fine. That's why we brought them."

It would be a while before the food arrived. So it seemed like as good a time as any for opening the presents. "Now, please."

"That's what I thought you'd say." Jackson's smile widened as he reached for the brightly wrapped box.

They'd been very quiet about what my present was going to be. I hadn't been expecting anything. So when Jackson started smiling and telling me he had a secret, I'd been surprised. I guess I shouldn't have been. Jackson liked doing little things for us. I just couldn't figure out what could be in the package.

It looked like one of those long rectangular boxes that pajamas would come in at Christmas.

Everyone was quiet as I turned the box over in my hands. I felt something shift, so I knew it couldn't be clothing. Thank goodness. There hadn't been any big gift-giving holidays since we'd met, so I hadn't seen what kind of shopper he was yet.

Sawyer leaned in closer, and he seemed to be vibrating with excitement. "Don't just look at it. Open it."

Part of me wanted to rip it open, but part of me wanted to savor it. It was my first birthday present from Jackson. They said they'd picked it out together, but the little looks Sawyer had given him made it clear whose idea it was.

"Don't rush me. It's my birthday." I'd been using that excuse all day long for just about everything.

Time to do the dishes? Nope, it's my birthday.

Aren't you going to eat something healthy for breakfast? Nope, it's my birthday.

I loved birthdays.

I was nearly bouncing in my chair by the time I peeled back the paper. I'd been right. It was one of those shirt boxes. But as I opened it, it became clear there wasn't just clothing inside.

There were papers.

There were also a few small presents wrapped up in tissue paper and a T-shirt that I couldn't see the logo on, but it was the paperwork that caught my eye first. What could they have picked out? Contrary to Jackson's worries, I wasn't old enough to be excited about stocks or something like that for my birthday.

"What is it?" The anticipation was still there but now I was confused.

Jackson and Sawyer both nearly giggled. Sawyer poked my arm and nodded toward the box. "Just look at it."

He was still ridiculously excited, so the chances of it being something financial went down dramatically, but I still wasn't sure what it could be. As I reached into the box and lifted out the paperwork, Sawyer seemed to be holding his breath. The blank sides were up, teasing me more, but as I turned them over, I knew exactly what it was.

"Universal Studios!" Laughter rumbled around the table as I started looking at our vacation. There was information about the tickets and even the hotel where we would be staying. We were going on vacation to Orlando. "This is fabulous. Thank you."

I gave each of them a kiss on the cheek and squeezed Jackson's hand. "We're going to go on vacation."

After a quick round of comments about how much fun it was going to be from Jackson's parents and some jealousy from Melissa, I opened the little presents. They'd gotten me a Harry Potter picture frame and notepad for my office, along with a T-shirt from the movie. I couldn't wait to get a picture taken of all three of us to put inside of the frame.

I looked back down at the papers. "When do you think we can go?"

"We need to wait until you're between classes, but other than that, I think we can work around your schedule." He smiled and leaned over and kissed my cheek. "I'm glad you're excited."

"It's wonderful." I was going to be saying that for weeks, but it was true.

Charlotte and Daniel smiled as they handed their box across the table. Daniel cautioned me as he held it out. "Be careful. It's heavier than it looks."

He was right. It wasn't quite bricks, but it was heavier than I'd have expected for a birthday present. I scooted back from the large round table and set the present on my lap. As I opened it, Charlotte spoke. "It's not quite an amusement park, but it's practical and enjoyable."

My brain started imagining dirtier things than she'd probably intended. My idea of practical and enjoyable was probably different from theirs. But I couldn't wait to see what they'd got me. "My own tools."

When Daniel had realized that Sawyer and I didn't have

any tools, he'd been stunned. He'd looked shocked when I'd said that we didn't have a screwdriver because most things could be opened with a butter knife.

Clearly, he'd wanted to remedy that situation. "Thank you."

From the packaging, I could see that there were a variety of tools. The box contained screwdrivers and some kind of electronic multi-tool that had different attachments. I had a feeling Daniel was going to have a field day showing me how all of it worked.

The best part was, they were purple.

Daniel started explaining how he knew that Jackson had his own tools, but Daniel made it clear that he thought everyone should have their own. As he kept talking, he explained that they were like clothes, where you got more comfortable with your own than using someone else's.

The whole thing sounded a little ridiculous, because I liked wearing Jackson's clothes, but I was touched.

The idea of Daniel wearing Charlotte's clothes was interesting. They probably wouldn't fit, though.

"Everybody in the family gets their own tools when they move out. We're a little late getting your set, but better late than never." I wasn't sure if Daniel meant that they were late because I'd already moved out of my parents' house or because I'd already moved in with Jackson. Either way, it was wonderful.

It was their way of showing me, and really, both Sawyer and me, that we were part of the family.

Giving the tools to Sawyer for a moment, I went around the table and gave both of them a hug. By the time I got back to my seat, it was Melissa's turn to be grinning like a lunatic. When she handed an envelope across the table, I knew from her expression it wasn't just a gift card.

"Thank you." As I opened the envelope and slid out the card, my curiosity started to build. Yes, there were a couple of scratch-off tickets and a good-sized gift card in it, but the note was what made me smile.

After wishing me happy birthday, Melissa had gone on to write that my real present was out in her car. She went on to tease that she had a variety of books she thought I would like and even said that one of them was hers, but she wasn't going to say which.

"This is wonderful, thank you. If I hit it big on the tickets, I'm not going to share, though." I held out the card so everyone could see and thanked Melissa again for the gift. As I tucked the envelope away in the box from Jackson and Sawyer, I saw Sawyer giving me a curious look. I just winked at him and mouthed, *Later*.

There was no way I was going to be the one to start that discussion in front of Jackson's parents.

But once they began discussing the elephant, I was going to have fun with it. The whole thing would be too funny to ignore. And if I played my cards right, I could end up getting a spanking for being naughty too.

"THAT WAS DELICIOUS. YOU DID A WONDERFUL JOB." Charlotte was all smiles as she finished up the last of her cheesecake.

In the past, everyone had gone over to their house for dessert after the birthday dinner, but when Jackson explained that I'd wanted to learn how to make a cheesecake, they'd been fine with the change. I was glad that it had turned out okay, and we only got a little lecture about cutting into it before everyone else arrived.

"Thank you." Between the balloons and the cheesecake, it actually felt like a real party. I'd even managed to get Sawyer into a birthday hat. "I'm just glad it turned out edible."

Sawyer had been right; the consistency had been weird. But it had turned out perfectly. I still thought that taste testing before everyone arrived had been a good idea. I'd have died if it had been gross.

And who wanted to wait all day long for dessert?

As Charlotte helped clean up the kitchen, she set everything down on the counter by the sink and came over to give me a hug. "Happy birthday, Cooper. I'm very glad that Jackson found you both. I hope you had a wonderful birthday."

I returned the hug before she stepped away. Smiling, I nodded. "It was a wonderful birthday. Thank you for celebrating with me."

I couldn't remember ever having a birthday as happy as that one.

My first birthday with Sawyer, once we were a family, had been incredibly special. But this one was just filled with happiness and laughter. They'd accepted us as part of their family, even though we were probably very different from what they'd expected.

After more hugs and a quick goodbye, Daniel and Charlotte left, claiming it was getting late for them, but there was something about the way Charlotte looked at Melissa that made me curious. Melissa hung back, telling them goodbye and saying she'd leave in a few minutes, but Charlotte just smiled and said she was sure she'd see Melissa soon.

As soon as their car drove away, and they headed toward the main road, I bounced up and down. "Where are my books? You made me wait forever. That's just mean."

Melissa laughed but grabbed her keys off the table and headed for her car. "There was no way I was going to give these to you in front of my parents. I don't care if they actually know what I write—it's still weird."

"No, what's weird is that none of you are willing to talk about it."

She shrugged as she opened the trunk of her car. "Personally, I'm pretty content pretending they don't know." She slammed the trunk and headed for the house, carrying a big decorative bag.

"I don't think your mother will be willing to let it go on forever. One of these days she's going to show up on your doorstep and get it all out in the open." And from the look on her face as they'd left the house, it probably wouldn't be as far into the future as Melissa hoped. Nope, her mother had the same glint in her eyes that she'd had at the barbecue.

"That's just mean." She frowned and gave me a dirty look. "Don't wish that on me."

"It's not going to be my fault when she shows up at your house. You should hide things better or talk about it and just get it over with. Now hurry, I've been waiting hours for these." Teasing me with the books and then making me wait all night for them was wrong.

Melissa laughed, clearly not worried about driving me crazy. "Here you go. Most of them are books I picked up at some conventions. So a lot of them are actually signed. I'm not going to tell you which one mine is or if it's signed or not. And if you guess, I don't want to know."

I snatched the bag from her hand gleefully and danced toward the living room. Sawyer and Jackson were trying to herd the balloons back into one corner as I skidded to a halt. "My books!"

Sawyer turned with an excited look on his face. He gave up trying to wrangle the balloons and walked over to me. "Let me see."

I clutched the bag to my chest and shook my head. "It's my present. I get to look first."

He stuck his tongue out at me, and his hands moved like he was going to tickle me. In trying to jump back out of his reach, I dropped the bag. Sawyer snatched it out of the air and laughed. "Tough luck, birthday boy."

"Hey!"

Sawyer's grin widened as he went over to the couch. I followed him, pouting, but when he started laying the books out on the table, I forgot to be frustrated with him. There was a variety of fetishes and topics, but all of them were gay romance novels. I couldn't wait to dig in and see which one she'd written.

Overwhelmed by the number of choices, I picked one at random and began reading the description on the back. As Jackson and Melissa talked, I kept going through the books. Some seemed to be sweet and others looked like they would be much hotter, but they all looked like fun.

Two of them were even about puppy play.

When I finally looked up from my treasures, I found everyone smiling at me. "Thank you! These are wonderful."

"Some of them I've read and some of them are new to me." Melissa pointed to one of the books with a sad-looking guy on the cover. "That one looked so good, I bought a copy for myself."

I grinned. "So I can assume that one's not yours?"

She laughed and nodded. "But I'm not going to tell you any more."

"I have my ways of making you talk. I'll figure it out."

She blushed a little bit and shook her head. "The deal was, you're not supposed to let me know if you guess."

"I don't remember ever agreeing to that." Just because that was what she wanted didn't mean it was what she would get. I wasn't going to encourage the elephants any more than they had already.

Melissa clearly hoped I wouldn't figure it out, but I thought she was ready to stop hiding. She wouldn't have given me one of her books otherwise. I stood and walked around the table to give her a hug. "Thank you for the books."

"You're welcome." As we stepped back from the hug, she gave Jackson a wicked grin. "You're going to have your hands full. Some of those books are going to be fabulous for his imagination."

Jackson rolled his eyes and seemed to be trying not to get embarrassed. "Thanks, Mellie."

She beamed at him. "You're welcome."

On any other night, I would have made her stay, so I could hear about how her work was actually going. But I hadn't forgotten Jackson's teasing promise of a surprise. "We're going to have to go to lunch this week. I want to hear about the new release."

She nodded. "Yes, let me look at my schedule, and I'll text you tomorrow."

"Perfect."

"All right, you guys have a good night." She gathered up her stuff and started walking to the kitchen.

"I know the polite thing to do is to offer you some dessert to take with you, but I'm going to keep it." I was not going to feel guilty about that.

Melissa laughed. "I don't blame you. I'd have kept it too."

"Because it was delicious." I did a not-so-subtle happy dance as we went through the kitchen. I'd made cheesecake.

Jackson and Sawyer called out from the living room as Melissa was leaving. I barely managed to hold in my excitement. I wanted to tell her that Jackson had a surprise for us, but I wasn't sure how that would make him feel. But I thought it was something he would consider more personal, and I didn't want to frustrate him.

When she was in her car and pulling away, I shut the door, locking it. Running through the kitchen, I threw myself into Jackson's arms. "Is it time for our surprise?"

20

SAWYER

COOPER'S EXCITEMENT WAS INFECTIOUS. I'd been as curious about Jackson's surprise as he'd been, but seeing the joy that poured out of him brought it all rushing back. Jackson pretended to give him a hesitant look. "I don't know. You've already gotten a lot of things today. Maybe I should wait until tomorrow."

Cooper didn't have to pause to think up a good argument. "But what about Sawyer? It's his turn for a surprise. Making him wait would just be mean, and he might get sad."

He gave Jackson his best wide-eyed expression and glanced over at me, looking pathetic. "You don't want to make Sawyer sad, do you?"

Jackson didn't seem to mind the manipulation. He gave Cooper an understanding nod and seemed to think about it like it was a rational argument. "I guess you're right. We shouldn't make Sawyer upset."

Cooper could barely contain his glee. It nearly burst out of him like an orgasm full of unicorns and glitter. "Thank you!"

"All right, you boys go jump in bed and wait for me. I'll

bring your surprise in there." Jackson gave Cooper's ass a smack as the bouncy nut made a mad dash for the bedroom.

Cooper paused long enough to grab my hand before dragging us at full speed to the bed. He jumped on the mattress with such force, he went bouncing to the other side, nearly falling off. Giggling, he threw himself onto the pillows, so worked up he was nearly vibrating. "What do you think it is?"

I shrugged. "I don't want to guess. Not knowing is half the fun."

Cooper gave a dramatic sigh and flopped backward on the bed again. "Guessing is the best part. You're crazy."

Before I could respond, we heard Jackson walking down the hallway. Cooper popped up from the pillows and sat up on his knees excitedly. His pup was so close to the surface I could almost see a tail wagging even though he was fully clothed. Trying not to laugh at his antics, I focused on Jackson.

He was nearly as excited as Cooper.

"Are you ready? Cooper, it sounded like you were getting in trouble." Jackson grinned at Cooper's frantic denial. His head was going back and forth so quickly, it looked like it might pop off.

"No, I've been good. What's the surprise, Master?" He bounced and wiggled as Jackson walked toward the bed.

As Jackson got closer, he pulled a rectangular box from behind his back. It was wrapped in silver paper and looked like another one of the clothing boxes we'd used to wrap Cooper's birthday present. I was beginning to get an idea of what might be in the box and from the excited little noises Cooper made, I had a feeling he suspected as well.

Jackson kicked off his shoes and climbed up onto the bed. Setting the box in front of him, he pulled us into his arms. Curling up beside him, we waited quietly while we stared at the box. Jackson took a moment to collect his thoughts, and the silence was almost deafening.

"When you let me into your family, one of the things you shared with me was how you felt about your collars." Jackson nodded as Cooper reached out with one hand and traced the edges of the package almost like he would touch one of us.

"You said you'd always imagined that your master would give you new collars once you found the right man." Jackson gave my arm a nudge, and I reached out to carefully open the package with Cooper's help.

Jackson smiled as we methodically opened the paper. "I started thinking about collars for you the first time I saw Cooper as a pup. As I watched Cooper play and you curled up beside me, Sawyer, I knew I wanted to be the man who would give you those collars."

He paused as we finally took the wrapping off. When he didn't give any hint about what we should do, Cooper and I paused, our hands on the box but not opening it. "Maybe I should've waited longer, or maybe I should've done this sooner. I don't know. But I don't want to continue building our life as a family without you knowing how much you mean to me."

A nod and a tender smile had us carefully lifting the lid off the box. "I want you to understand how much I love you and how much being your master means to me every time you see the collars. I never imagined that this was how my life would turn out, but I couldn't have asked for a better family. You both mean the world to me, and I can't wait to see where our life goes from here."

Jackson moved his arms from around us and reached into the box to pick up our collars. Holding out the two leather circles, he gave us a tender smile. It was easy to see which collar was intended for me and which one for Cooper even without seeing our tags. They were both very similar, but it was clear Jackson wanted to show our personalities in them.

They were beautifully made.

The dark brown leather looked soft and supple. They were

both decorated with little paw prints that were set into the leather. Cooper's were done in a rainbow of colors that were set into it and made the little paw prints stand out.

Mine had the same design, but instead of the bright colors, it was done in silver to match my tag. It wasn't until they got closer that I saw the delicate M that was in between the paws. I wasn't sure if it was intentional or not, but to me, it looked like no matter how the collar was worn, Master would always be surrounded by his pups. It was the perfect symbol of our life together.

"My sweet boys, my loving pups, will you wear my collars?"

The words were so tender and loving that I wanted to give him the perfect response.

Cooper didn't need perfection. He just wanted to let Jackson know how much he loved him. Our loving goofball threw himself into Jackson's arms, grinning like a lunatic. "Yes!"

Jackson's laughter was loving and warm as he gave Cooper a smacky kiss. "I love you, nut."

Then, Jackson looked over at me, and I nodded. Curling into him even closer, I reached out and traced one finger along the collar. It was the softest leather I'd ever felt, and I knew how much care had gone into it. Tilting my head up, I gave Jackson a tender kiss. "Yes, Master, I would love to wear your collar."

"Thank you. I love you." Jackson pressed another kiss to my lips before easing back to look at the box on the bed. "I have one more surprise for you both."

Cooper's whole body gave another excited wiggle and he just about threw himself into Jackson's lap. "Another present?"

Laughing, Jackson nodded. "Yes."

Jackson reached into the box and picked up a piece of tissue paper off the bottom of the box. I couldn't see what it had been covering up, but Cooper just melted. "Oh, Master."

Leaning closer so I could see, I felt the same rush of emotion as Cooper. It was two thin necklaces with tiny locks instead of clasps. Jackson picked one up and brought it over to my neck. Pausing, he waited until I nodded before opening the little hidden clasp that released the lock. As he put it around my neck, he smiled and had a faraway look in his eyes.

When it was fastened, he leaned in and kissed my cheek. "It should be thin enough that no one will see it under your clothes, but I wanted to give you something you could wear every day. Not a lock where I have the key, but a lock where you're choosing to keep me wrapped around you."

I felt tears prickling in my eyes, but I nodded and threw my arms around him in a tight hug. "It's perfect."

"Me too!" Cooper's excitement came out in a rush as he bounced closer.

Jackson chuckled. "You too?"

"Yes!" Nearly vibrating with anticipation, Cooper barely held it together as Jackson took his time putting the second necklace around his neck.

When it was finished, Cooper gave him a quick kiss then jumped off the bed and dashed over to the dresser. Admiring it in the mirror, and probably himself wearing it, Cooper beamed. "It's perfect!"

Jackson moved the box out of the way and wrapped himself around me, smiling at Cooper. "I'm glad you like it."

Cooper bounced back over to us and climbed up, throwing himself over us. "It's perfect and fabulous and it's a collar I can wear all the time!"

Cooper wiggled and grinned as we wrapped our arms around him to keep him still. Trying not to laugh, because that would just egg him on, I tried to pin him down. "You've had too much sugar."

That worked like a light switch to turn off the drama. Suddenly he was sweet and calm. "No, I haven't."

Someone clearly wanted to make sure he got more dessert later.

Jackson chuckled. "I don't know. You seem slightly hyper to me."

Cooper gave Jackson a wide-eyed stare, blinking down at him with an innocent-looking pout. "I'm just excited."

The way his hips flexed, I knew Jackson was getting a very good example of just how *excited* Cooper was. Jackson's voice dipped lower. "Excited for your collar or for something else?"

Cooper's coy smile had my cock jerking. "Can't it be both, Master?"

Jackson shifted, and his hand must have slid down Cooper's body to cup his ass, because Cooper moaned and thrust his hips forward again. "Please, Master."

Jackson seemed to have decided to give Cooper exactly what he wanted, because he moved again, and Cooper gasped and whimpered. Jackson chuckled. "Is that what you're hinting at?"

Whatever he'd done had been perfect according to Cooper because he nodded and melted into us. Jackson shifted so that Cooper slid down between us to the mattress. Cooper turned over and reached out to pull us into a hug. "I love you both so much."

Jackson and I gave him matching kisses to his cheeks and gave him back the sweet words he'd given us. Jackson looked over at me with a knowing smile and started kissing down Cooper's neck. Following his signal, I started licking and nibbling down the other side so Cooper was writhing and making low begging sounds.

When we reached his shoulders, Jackson sat up and glanced over at me. "I think he's wearing too many clothes. What do you think?"

I'd agree to whatever got us naked the fastest. Cooper

wasn't the only one who was excited. "I think you're right, Master."

Jackson's heated smiled turned tender, and he leaned over Cooper to give me a kiss. Cooper sighed. "You two are so sexy together."

I chuckled as Jackson finally pulled away. "If he can talk in full sentences, I don't think we've been giving him enough attention."

"Oh yes, I think you're right." Jackson looked down at Cooper and gave him a heated look. "It might take us a while to make sure he's had enough."

Another shiver raced through Cooper, and he couldn't seem to decide if he wanted to say thank you or if he wanted to force us to hurry. Luckily, it wasn't for him to decide. Jackson reached out and started working Cooper's shirt up his body. "Let's get this off you."

Helping Jackson, we had Cooper's shirt off in seconds with Cooper stretched out on the bed, curious to see what would happen next. I thought Jackson might want to finish getting Cooper naked, but instead, he pointed to the bed next to Cooper. "I want you to stretch out beside him. With each of us taking a nipple, we'll have to see how much *attention* we can give him."

An excited whimper escaped Cooper as we lay down beside him. Taking one nipple between my lips, I plucked at it and began sucking on the sensitive bud. Cooper started to moan again, but when Jackson started flicking the other nipple tenderly with just the tip of his tongue, Cooper couldn't seem to decide what to do.

As we teased and played with Cooper's body, going back and forth between licking his nipples and nibbling on them while he writhed, we watched as he started to come undone. But Jackson didn't seem to be ready to let Cooper off so easily.

When Cooper's nubs were puffy and well-loved, Jackson

started kissing his way down Cooper's chest. Following his lead, I licked over Cooper's ribs and down to his hip that was barely covered by his pants.

Jackson sat up and gave me another nod. It was finally time for Cooper to get naked. With the two of us working together, we had him stripped in seconds while Cooper wiggled and shoved to hurry us along, desperate to give us more to touch and taste.

Instead of laying him flat and going straight for Cooper's dick, Jackson rolled Cooper on his side and had him prop one leg up. With Cooper's tempting ass on display for me, I knew what Jackson had in mind. Jackson wasn't going to make him guess, though. "We're going to have so much fun with you. I'm going to keep you nice and hard while Sawyer gets you ready. You want to feel our dicks sliding deep inside you, don't you?"

"Fuck. Together?" Cooper's eyes went wide, but he didn't say no, which made me smile.

Jackson look startled but recovered quickly. Evidently, that wasn't where his mind had gone. They were so funny. "Not yet, but if that's something you want, we can talk about it."

Stretching up, Jackson gave Cooper a scorching kiss. Oh yes, they were both having fun imagining that fantasy. When Jackson finally pulled away, he lay down on the bed so his head was at Cooper's dick.

Cooper's fantasy about having both cocks must have been good because as Jackson started licking the head of Cooper's dick and I kneaded at his cheeks, Cooper moaned and jerked. Jackson gave a low chuckle, and I just spread him open even more because I knew how much Cooper liked being on display.

The gasp of pleasure from Cooper let me know the moment when Jackson finally took him completely in his mouth. When I started circling Cooper's tight ring of muscles and flicking my tongue over it, he whined and writhed. He couldn't seem to decide what he wanted more, but since it wasn't up to him and he didn't have to choose, I didn't see the problem. He just had to feel and remember not to come until he had permission.

That was going to be harder than he imagined, though.

As I flicked my tongue and squeezed his cheeks, Cooper made the most beautiful sounds. He wanted it too much to let his body guard against me, so it wasn't long until the muscles relaxed and I was fucking him with my tongue, kissing and stabbing it in as far as it would go. It was just enough to make him beg for more, but not enough to satisfy him.

"Please...Jackson...Sawyer...please...I...I'm..." His stuttered, broken words were music to Jackson, who hummed again with pleasure. It egged him on and pushed him to take Cooper even closer to the edge.

When Cooper's body was open for me and frantically trying to pull me deeper, I brought one finger up and started fucking him with just the tip. Cooper started trying to desperately shove himself back and forth to get more from each of us, but Jackson's tight grip on Cooper's hip made it almost impossible.

The rising desperation in his voice made me realize that no matter how long we wanted to pleasure him and torture him, his pleas for more would eventually push Jackson to give in. Reaching behind me to the nightstand, I grabbed the lube and brought it over to the bed.

Cooper was too distracted by Jackson's mouth and the little tip of my finger that was teasing his hole, so when I pulled out to slick up my fingers, he didn't seem to realize what was happening.

"Sawyer...don't stop...fuck...more...Sawyer!" I just chuckled as I brought my slicked finger back to his opening and sank deep with one thrust.

It was just a single finger, but Cooper cried out like it was the thickest dick he'd ever taken and another shiver raced through him as he desperately tried to chase his orgasm. Jackson wasn't ready to let Cooper orgasm yet, however, and did something to Cooper's dick that made him gasp and shake before thrusting his hips forward. "Please, Jackson, again. Fuck, again."

Chuckling low, Jackson did whatever it was again, and Cooper whimpered but clenched down on my finger like pleasure was flooding through him. I couldn't wait to figure out what Jackson had done to get such a fabulous response from Cooper.

"Don't forget, pup. You don't get to come until I say so. Remember?" Jackson's low words made my cock even harder, and even though I knew he was talking to Cooper, all I wanted to do was to promise to do whatever he said.

Cooper beat me to it, though. "Yes...remember... good...please...now..."

Jackson's arm moved, and I pictured him slowly jerking Cooper off because Cooper whimpered again as Jackson told him how good he was being and how Jackson was having fun playing with him. Unable to resist the temptation, I pulled almost all the way out of Cooper's body before adding a second finger.

There was no way we'd last much longer.

He gasped and whined before trying to push me deeper. Jackson just made a low, pleased sound, and his head dipped back to Cooper's dick. As I stretched Cooper, and Jackson had fun wringing frantic, pleasured cries from him, we both pushed him higher and higher.

When I had three fingers in, and he was more than ready, Jackson must have finally realized that Cooper holding back his orgasm by a thread, because he moved away from Cooper's cock and nodded at me.

Thank god.

Pulling my fingers out, I shoved my clothes off while Cooper shook and Jackson grinned at the two of us. He wasn't much smoother, though. Jackson's hands jerked, and even through his pants I could see he was hard as a rock and desperate to slide into Cooper.

When we were both naked, I slicked my cock before reaching over to take Jackson's dick in my hand to ready him. He was hard and hot and I could feel the blood pumping through him as I dragged the lube across his skin. He groaned, but thrust his dick forward to let me get him ready.

"Lie down beside him, Sawyer." Jackson's words startled me and had me pulling back. I was going to get to fuck Cooper?

"Yes, Master." Cooper and Jackson both gave low moans as I whispered the words and stretched out behind Cooper, my cock teasing at his needy hole.

Jackson lay in front of Cooper and positioned his arm under Cooper's leg to open him even more. Once I saw Jackson move, I knew what he wanted. So did Cooper, because he started jerking back and forth between us, mumbling low. "Thank you...fuck...yes...thank you...fuck..."

I couldn't even laugh or respond. Everything in me was focused on Jackson's face and the wonderful men stretched out in front of me. When Jackson leaned over Cooper and kissed my lips, I wanted to come right then.

"My beautiful boys. Show Cooper how much you want him and how much you love him, Sawyer." Jackson's sexy, sweet words had my cock throbbing, and I sank into Cooper in one slow thrust.

Cooper cried out, and the rambling mess of *thank yous* and *fucks* continued as he shook and waited for me to move. When I didn't go fast enough, he thrust back and whimpered for more. My first response was to give him whatever he wanted, but Jackson reached over and put a hand on my hip. "Slowly. He's going to have to wait."

Jackson was going to kill us.

Cooper seemed to think so too because the *fucks* he was mumbling took a more frustrated turn. But Jackson just chuckled and used his hand to guide my body, which was sexy as hell and had me fighting to remember I couldn't come either.

Not until Master had given me permission.

That thought made me jerk and my cock sank roughly into Cooper. He sighed, but Jackson shook his head. "No, remember the rules."

"Slowly. Yes. Slowly." Fuck, I was turning into Cooper.

Jackson let me make love to Cooper with tortuously slow thrusts for a few more seconds before his hand stilled me. "Now it's my turn."

Fuck. We were taking turns.

Pulling out slowly, I watched as Jackson moved lower and repositioned Cooper so he could sink into Cooper's tight heat. Watching Jackson's cock gradually enter Cooper was almost as hot as being able to feel Cooper's body wrapped around mine.

Almost.

It was also maddeningly erotic and so frustrating I wanted to jack myself off and come all over Cooper's back. That wasn't the plan, though. Jackson kept up the measured pace for a few long minutes before withdrawing. "Sawyer, again."

If I was frustrated, then Cooper was almost insane. He shook and begged and sighed in relief when I started easing into him, but the careful pace just made him more frantic. Jackson kept up the sexy rounds of painfully slow lovemaking until Cooper was a whimpering mess and little shocks of pleasure he could barely hold back kept firing through him.

When Jackson leaned over and kissed me, I almost missed the low words he whispered. "Come, my love."

The words finally cleared the hazy fog in my brain and my hips shot forward with a mind of their own. Cooper had gotten so used to the gentle in and out that as I started to fuck him hard, he wasn't sure what to do. Before he could come, my orgasm burst through me and I shot deep inside him.

Jackson leaned down and I distantly heard him whispering

to Cooper about how we were going to mark him and fill him up with our cum. The dirty words were said with such love it only made them hotter. As I finally pulled out, I gave Jackson a kiss on the cheek and fell back onto the mattress. I felt flattened, but they weren't done yet.

I watched as Jackson growled and rolled a desperate Cooper onto his back. Jackson pushed into him in one deep, hard thrust and must have nailed Cooper's prostate because he screamed out and cum shot out in long ribbons onto his chest. Neither seemed interested in the fact that Cooper hadn't gotten permission to come. Jackson would remember eventually and Cooper would just love it.

Jackson couldn't hold back once he felt Cooper pulse and tighten around him, because he quickly followed Cooper with shaking, straining thrusts. When the last aftershocks had faded from Cooper and he just lay almost comatose on the bed, Jackson stilled over him and carefully pulled out.

Lying down beside Cooper, Jackson gave him a tender kiss, whispering quietly, before stretching over to kiss me. "I love you both more than I ever thought possible. Thank you for coming into my life."

Pouring every ounce of love I felt for him into his kiss, I wrapped my arms around him and held him tight. "Thank you for opening your heart and realizing what was possible."

As much as I loved Jackson, I knew without Cooper it never would have been possible. Cooper's earnest belief that we would find a master and make a family with him one day had kept us going through long nights and times when I wasn't sure how we would make it. There'd been times when that faith, and my desperation to keep him from losing it, had been the only thing that kept me getting out of bed in the morning.

There was no place else I'd rather be and no one else I wanted to call Master. We might have found him by accident, but it had been fate that pulled us together.

ABOUT MA INNES

M.A. Innes is the pseudonym for best-selling author Shaw Montgomery. While Shaw writes femdom and m/m erotic romance. M.A. Innes is the side of Shaw that wants to write about topics that are more taboo. If you liked the book, please leave a short review. It is greatly appreciated.

Do you want to join the newsletter? Help with character names and get free sneak peeks at what's coming up? Just click on the link.

https://my.publishingspark.com/join/?show=239

You can also get information on upcoming books and ideas on Shaw's website.

www.authorshawmontgomery.com

You can also join me in my readers group on Facebook.

https://www.facebook.com/groups/shawsplayroom/

Made in the USA
Middletown, DE
05 November 2018